TANGO

THE RANGER

--- PULLING THREADS ---

Book Eleven

SHERYLL O'BRIEN

This is a work of fiction. All characters in this book are the product of an overactive imagination. Any businesses, organizations, places, events, and incidents are used fictionally. Any resemblance to a real person, living or dead, is a tremendous coincidence.

ISBN 978-1-939351-30-2

Printed in United States of America

Mom,

I write them.
I print them.
I deliver them.
And you read them because you love me.
That is so sweet.

I publish them.
I deliver them.
And you read them because you love them.
This is so wonderful.

ACKNOWLEDGMENT

Donna Eaton, aka Donna Davenport. Thank you from the whole of my heart – for reading and rereading my words – for encouraging me to do this for me – for keeping the pressure on to deliver more and more stories – and for being my best friend.

A heartfelt thank you to my team:

Andria Flores ~ Editor extraordinaire.
Nancy Pendleton ~ Goddess of the publishing world.
Jessica Champion ~ Web designer and manager.
25 Hours Consulting
Daryl Bruinsma ~ Cover Design & Animation.

Testimonials

"One book will set the hook!" ~ Nancy Pendleton

"This avid reader predicts that Sheryll O'Brien will become your favorite author. She's mine." ~ Ruth S. Bodreau

"The characters draw you in immediately. You will worry, laugh, hope, and love right along with them." ~ Donna Eaton

"There is nothing sweeter than a Sunday morning coffee, a blanket, overcast skies, and a *Pulling Threads* novel." ~ Andria Flores

"Everything you'd want in a good book. Humor, romance, suspense and great characters! It even takes place by the ocean! Loved it." ~ Helena Green

"I could write a book about the wonderfulness of it all." ~ Faith Lavallee

"Hunks, humor, and heartache! What more could you ask for?" ~ Marjorie McCarthy

"*Bullet Bungalow* is a page turning family saga and then *Netti Barn* and *Cutters Cove* come along and add a whole lot of trauma to the drama." ~ Jessica O'Brien

"The most promising new author I've encountered in my publishing career!" ~ Jim P. - Woodwind Press

--- Pulling Threads ---

Bullet Bungalow
Netti Barn
Cutters Cove
They Run
They Hide
They Choose

PENOBSCOT BAY
A Rocco Fiancetti Incorporated Investigation

Reasons
Rescues
Resolutions
Torment
Tango

Coming soon...

Tests
Resolve
Revenge
Rebound

--- Twisted Threads ---

Coming soon...

Her Scream
Stay Safe

Dead Women Don't Talk

Abigail

He straddled her chest locking her arms beneath his knees and silencing her with a hand to her mouth. He put a loaded gun to her head, "If you make a sound, I will kill you. Do you understand?"

She nodded.

"I came to deliver a message. You need to listen to everything I have to say. I am going to gag you and tape your mouth shut. I will not hurt you if you cooperate. Do you understand?"

She nodded—opened her mouth—moaned pitifully.

He put a pair of silk panties in—taped her mouth shut—exhaled fully.

"Open your eyes, Abigail. Very good. Turner Rodgers does not want you in DC. He is taking back his block. Do you understand?"

She nodded.

"The Realm wants you dead."

Celia

He straddled her chest locking her arms beneath his knees and silencing her with a hand to her mouth. He put a loaded gun to her head.

"If you make a sound, I will kill you. Do you understand?"

She nodded.

"I came to deliver a message. You need to listen to everything I have to say. I am going to gag you and tape your mouth shut. I will not hurt you if you cooperate. Do you understand?"

She nodded—opened her mouth—whimpered pitifully.

He put a pair of silk panties in—taped her mouth shut—exhaled fully.

"Open your eyes, Celia. Very good. The Realm does not want you talking to the Feds about Tango. Do you understand?"

She nodded.

"The Realm wants you dead."

Dominique

He handed off a vial of poison. This is for prisoner BOP-PA-555925. From outside LewPen he sent the message, "The Realm wants you dead."

Tango

Sam Adams seals the deal.

Manuel Xavier and Fred Serpico, lead detectives for Rocco Fiancetti Incorporated, are elbow deep in filing cabinets that line the walls of Abigail Forrester's home office when Manuel's cell rings. He considers ignoring the call—considers otherwise when he sees it's the new mayor of Lewisburg calling.

"Hello, Mr. Mayor."

"Manuel, have you heard the news about Dominique?"

"What news?"

"I'm sorry, Manuel. Dominique was murdered in her cell at LewPen."

Manuel runs to the living room, turns on the television, and watches the breaking news report.

> **"... Dominique Brettenvue, female member of the criminal organization known as The Realm was found murdered in her cell at Lewisburg Penitentiary earlier today. Sources say the suspected cause of death is poisoning. Brettenvue began serving a life-sentence after pleading guilty to state and federal charges and turning over evidence against other Realm leaders. It has been rumored that**

> **Antonio Alvarez, the de facto leader of the disbanded criminal enterprise known as The Realm, issued a kill order against Dominique Brettenvue several…"**

Within minutes of receiving Malcolm's call, Manuel receives one from FICA Director Stacy Remington. "Manuel, I assume you have heard about Dominique?"

"Yes, ma'am."

"I wanted to tell you myself, but I was unavoidably detained upstairs."

The former FBI agent knows that being 'unavoidably detained upstairs' is code for Stacy having just had her ass handed to her by the director of the FBI. He also knows that two murdered prosecution witnesses, one under federal protection, and one in a federal penitentiary, are **very** good reasons for the ass-reaming.

He treads lightly, "Will you be able to sit anytime soon, Director Remington?"

"Not likely. I need to meet with you and Fred Serpico as soon as possible. Does the death of Dominique factor into when that meeting can happen?"

"No, ma'am."

"Very well, I'll be in Philly tomorrow. Please put all of your efforts into getting as much information from the Forrester files as possible. Focus on the big players. I'm afraid your services may be terminated and the case kicked down the chain to the Philadelphia Police Department."

The implications of what is being said is huge. "I'll see you tomorrow, Director."

Fred, who heard parts of the conversation, asks, "We're off the case? Is that the gist of things?"

"Not yet. Stacy wants us to document as much information on the big players as we can before she gets here tomorrow. I already sent Abigail's financials to Leavy, so let's get to Abigail's office and take a shitload of pictures of file documents and send them to RFI for safe keeping."

Fred tosses a blonde wooden block to his partner, "Read the bottom."

"Benton Brettenvue."

"We need to disassemble the tower on Abigail's desk and take pictures of every damned block."

"Let's go."

As the men hightail it upstairs, Manuel finishes updating Fred on the remainder of the talk he had with his former boss, "Stacy said if we are removed from the case, it is going to be kicked down to the Philly PD. We should call Detective Brothers and have him come here later, see if he will keep us in the loop, after the fact."

"Speaking of after the fact, are you..."

"Can't go there about Dominique. Not now, Fred."

"When you can…"

"I know."

Philadelphia Detective, Ted Brothers, brings two large pizzas and a six pack of Sam Adams to the Forrester condo early evening. Manuel and Fred take that as a sign that Brothers might 'play nice'.

"The Forrester case is coming back to Philly," Brothers says off the top.

Fred takes point with the detective. "When?"

"Next day or two. I'm gonna grab it, but I'm guessing you already know that part and that's why I'm here."

Fred nods. "Someone doesn't want this mess figured out. No disrespect intended, Detective."

"None taken. The chances of me getting through the meat of this by myself is slim to none. Now, if I had an assist from a spy team like RFI, I might get the goods," Brothers lifts his bottle and takes a long pull of beer.

"We're pretty good in the assist department, Detective," Fred matches Brothers' pull.

The men let Sam Adams seal the deal with a clink of their bottles.

Spilling secrets.

Benton Brettenvue, shagger of the dead Abigail, husband of the dead Celia, and father of the dead Dominique, sits on an Adirondack rocker, on a tiny veranda, at a tiny motel, in Beaver Falls—a little hamlet tucked into the southwest corner of PA. He raises a cheap, motel room plastic cup toward the noisy, quick moving Beaver River, a mere stone's throw from where he sits. "Fuck you, bitches," he slurs the crude toast to the recently departed. Before swallowing the remainder of his whiskey, his thoughts turn to Granger Mitchell, "You spent an awful lot of time with Dominique and a fair amount of time with Celia. There are people who will be interested in knowing what you know—so you'd better watch your back, old man."

Philadelphia
Granger Mitchell, senior partner of Mitchell and Morgan, is sitting at his massive desk across from McKay Wallace, head of his criminal law division. The two have spent several minutes in stunned silence. Granger pushes himself off his chair and breaks the silence, "Abigail Forrester, Celia Brettenvue, and Dominique Brettenvue—all three women were murdered within a matter

of days of one another—all three women are intricately tied to one another."

McKay pushes in, "Two of those three women have been spilling secrets about some very powerful people. You and I are the only living secret keepers, now." There's a bit more silence after that unnecessary reminder.

After several minutes staring out his office window Granger cuts to the crux. "All three women are known associates of Benton Brettenvue, and to varying degrees, of Peruvian crime lord, Antonio Alvarez. Benton had personal cause to want the women dead, but the circumstances behind their murders are beyond Benton's capabilities. Whoever pulled this off wields a great deal of power. Alvarez has the power and resources, but it would be next to impossible to pull this off from inside the ADX Supermax Penitentiary. These women are dead because they knew too much. We should expect that the person or persons responsible for these murders are going to want to know what you and I learned from Celia and Dominique." Granger takes a minute to reconcile what he knows is the truth of the matter. "McKay, everything we know is housed in our offices, at the Carriage House on my estate, and in our memories. We need to protect our files, as well as ourselves and the people in our personal and professional lives."

McKay nods and leaves. "I'll go get my files."

Granger picks up his phone and places a call, shakes his head when it is answered.

"Yo!"

"Researcher Randy, this is Granger Mitchell."

"Pardons, Mr. Mitchell. Yo, sir."

"Randy, I need you in Philadelphia within the next few hours. Is that doable?"

"On my way, sir."

Granger places his next call to his son-in-law, the newly seated Mayor of Lewisburg. "Mr. Mayor, I hope I haven't caught you at a bad time."

"Not at all, Granger."

"As you know, my firm was representing and sequestering Celia Brettenvue at the time of her murder. I have also been meeting with Dominique Brettenvue at the penitentiary for the months preceding her murder. Both women have provided me with information that certain elements will want to keep quiet."

"The silencing efforts used thus far are very effective, Granger—and cause for concern."

"...which brings me to the reason for this call. I have files. The information contained within those files needs to be protected. I have asked Researcher Randy to come to Philadelphia later today. My plan is for him to scan all of the documents relating to Dominique and Celia and send them into whatever portal in cyberland he deems appropriate. I would like your opinion about Randy's involvement in this situation, Malcolm, since there are inherent risks."

Malcolm's answer is quick in coming. "The Kid is working way beneath his skill set. I'm not sure why that is, Granger. We recently learned top law enforcement agencies, including RFI, want him on their payroll. Ultimately, this assignment is Randy's call, but I think he can handle anything that comes his way—of course, he'll handle it Randy-style."

"I suspect he will. Now that that's settled, how is our girl doing?"

Malcolm smiles wide, "Gretchen is in full word mashing mode going on about the smallest humans in the world requiring so much paraphernalia and wondering what makes us think she can do the whole mothering thing when she isn't sure she has ever held a baby and dithering about where we'll put DelRae when she gets here and … you get the drift. I can't help with *all* of Gretchen's concerns, but the placement of the baby is being taken care of. There's a work crew here building a nursery and playroom."

Granger laughs at Malcolm's mock of Gretchen, then cautions. "You know, Malcolm, the word mashes might be hereditary. Gretchen's mother was known to mash a few words from time to time."

"Better set yourself then for a mashing Miss DelRae Price, Grandpa."

"Better set yourself, Mr. Mayor."

Desperados and recently departed.

Researcher Randy works well into the night photocopying, scanning, and uploading files. Security staff informed him hours earlier that the law office was closed for the night and no one should be on the executive floors until morning rounds at 6 AM. Therefore, cause for concern is immediate when he hears footfalls nearing the executive suite.

Holed up in an interior photocopy room located just outside Granger's inner sanctum, Randy darkens the only light source inside the room—his computer and scanner. He holds his breath as footfalls near then move past. He waits until the visitors are through the double glassed doors of the executive suite, then quickly shoves his computer and case files into his messenger bag. He cracks open the photocopy room door, peeks out, waits until the beams of two flashlights move to the far end of the executive office, then slips from the room. He inches the full length of the hallway, momentarily pausing when he hears one of the flashlight-carrying-men yell, "Stop!"

Randy. Does. Not. Stop. He corners to the bank of elevators, pulls the fire alarm, and hops into an open vertical ride. The two gun-waving, ski-masked men push onto the stairway opposite the closing elevator door.

Resourceful Randy waits until the count of 'ten holy shits' before he opens the elevator door and heads back into the executive suite. While awaiting the arrival of building security and the fire department, Randy makes a phone call to Granger Mitchell. "Sorry for the lateness, sir, but I had some unexpected company this evening. Two gun-toting, would-be-file-absconders are currently fleeing the premises of your namesake firm. I expect the arrival of security and the fire department imminently and would appreciate your assist, so that I am not shot or hosed."

"I'm on it," Granger says before disconnecting.

The top floor of the Mitchell and Morgan Law Offices is ablaze with light when Granger and Faye Mitchell arrive shortly before 2 AM. The security officers who reluctantly resisted the urge to shoot Randy are standing sentry outside the inner sanctum. Granger and Faye go behind closed doors and find Randy sitting on the floor of Granger's office, legal documents and handwritten notes being photographed, scanned and uploaded at lightning speed.

Randy gives a, "Yo," and continues his work. When he is finished, he pops from the floor and wipes his forehead, "Phew, someone sure wants these files, sir. You were on the proactive side of things when you put me between the desperados and the words of the recently departed."

Granger nods at the kid, who is really a skinny-jean, plaid shirt, wool slouch, Vans wearing thirty-year-old hipster. Granger gets serious and asks, "The men, did they see you?"

Randy nods, "Couldn't be helped, sir, but the good news is they didn't shoot me, although the waving of their guns in my direction is a fair indicator that it was their plan."

Granger nods, a scowl of concern etching his face. "Since we have no way of knowing if they are in the vicinity, we can't let you go out into the night alone, Randy. Get your things, you can stay at our estate."

The Kid's wide smile fades quickly, "If it's all the same to you, sir, I don't think I'm all that comfortable staying at the Carriage House. The last tenant didn't fare so well."

"You'll stay at the Cottage with us."

"Now, that's a plan Researcher Randy can endorse. Let's go, Legal Beagle."

Granger growls at the term. "I believe the correct term is Legal Eagle."

Randy laughs, "You sound just like Mr. Mayor when you growl. Can't wait to tell Mrs. Mayor, although she won't believe me. Better record the next growl. You'll probably do it again before I leave, right, Legal Beagle?"

Granger nods, "Undoubtedly. Let's go."

275

Malcolm knocks on Randy's apartment door shortly before 7 AM. The renovation crew is expected, and he wants a few minutes with Randy before they arrive. He knuckle-wraps three times more before calling The Kid's name. When there isn't an answer, Malcolm gets concerned enough to place a phone call.

"Yo, it's early, 77."

"Where are you?" Malcolm growls.

"In your wife's bed."

"Kid, where the hell are you?" he growls again.

Randy laughs, "Seriously. The Legal Beagle and his Missus saved me from some gun-wielding, would-be-file-absconders last night at the law firm. They insisted I stay the night and gave me Gretchen's old room. Did you know your track and field woman ran her ass off in college? The walls and shelves are covered with medals, ribbons, and trophies."

"I knew some. She was good?"

"Damn 77, she was better than good. When we hang up, go introduce yourself to your woman, would ya?"

"I'll do that. When are you coming back?"

"My work is done, but senior partner thinks the rummagers will be watching my car."

"I'll ask Granger if you can borrow a corporate car. I need to talk to you about things when you get back. Find me."

Malcolm crawls back onto his bed and pulls his sleeping woman into his spoon. Gretchen moans as she pulls herself from sleep.

"I was having the most wonderful dream. DelRae was about nine months old, and she was sitting on your knee. She's all arms and legs moving about, and smiling this wide, near-toothless grin at her daddy. She's lighter skinned than you, but she favors you very much. She has a head full of black springy curls and the biggest round cornflower blue eyes. I'm telling you Malcolm; DelRae is the most beautiful thing in all the world. I just know that is what she looks like. I just know it."

Malcolm smiles against Gretchen's head, "Don't doubt it, Woman. Listen, when you come off this DelRae cloud, I want to talk to you about a couple things. Join me in the kitchen when you can."

"Good things or bad things? Because if it's bad things it will be awhile. I don't want to lose this happy place I'm in right now."

"Take your time, then."

The wife responds just as the husband expected she would, she makes a move to get up. "Need a lift, Woman?" He smiles wide as the pushing, grunting, and hoisting intensifies.

Gretchen throws an early morning set of daggers his way, then squeezes his offered hand. After the bed extracting, and glass of orange juice partaking, and baby girl inside her momma two-stepping, Malcolm leads Gretchen to their conversation couch which has been moved from the game room into the living room during the renovations. They sit together and watch the goings on at Hufnagle Park from the bank of windows at the far end of the penthouse.

Malcolm takes Gretchen's hand into his gigantic paw. "You will remain calm or I stop talking. There is an issue, but it is under control. Are we good here, Gretchen?"

She nods.

"Your father asked Randy to help him with a project in Philly, yesterday. As you know, Granger has been meeting with Dominique at the penitentiary for months, and he recently began representing Celia. He has a treasure trove of information from his meetings with the two women. He and McKay Wallace asked Randy to preserve the information by scanning it and securing it in cyberspace. While The Kid was working at the firm late last night, two men broke into the inner sanctum, presumably looking for the files. Randy heard them and was able to escape. Granger insisted that Randy stay with him and Faye at the Cottage. He will be back later today." Malcolm is holding Gretchen's wrist and feels her pulse pick up speed. He runs his thumb across her pulse point, "Are we still good, Gretchen?"

She nods.

"On a side note, I spoke with Manuel and Fred, yesterday. They are still in Philly investigating at the Forrester condo, though they expect to be removed from the case. When that happens, the murder investigations of Abigail and Celia will be handled by PPD. The RFI team thinks the move is an attempt to keep the cases from being solved. The implications of that are…."

"Staggering," Gretchen interrupts. "The implications of that are staggering."

Malcolm nods, "Apparently, Director Remington requested Manuel and Fred preserve as much information from the murder scenes, as possible." Malcolm checks in with his woman, "Are you still good, Gretchen?"

She nods.

"When RFI is removed from the case, Fred and Manuel are going rogue with their investigation. They want to bring Randy on board as an assist. If we have any objections to this, we need to raise them with Randy before their ask."

"I haven't any objections, Malcolm. He should be cautioned about where the legal lines are, but if he crosses them, I know a very good lawyer. As a matter of fact, I am a very good lawyer. Are we about finished here because I need to pee?"

Malcolm gets up and hoists his woman, “We’re done.”

Gretchen scurries away—as quickly as an eight-month pregnant woman can scurry, that is.

Know your audience.

Upon his return to 275, Randy prepares for his game of Hide 'n Seek. As it turns out, he does not have to **find** anyone. "Geez, Mr. Mayor. When you told me to find you, I was expecting a bona fide game of Hide 'n Seek. We should make note that you suck at hiding. It must be the height, or…"

Malcolm points to a chair, "Sit."

Randy sits, "That's some unwelcome bossiness."

"Randall."

"Wow, 77, you sound just like His Eminence, Judge Parker."

"I have no doubt your father spent some time lecturing you. It's my turn."

"Lecture? Damn, 77, no respectable Hide 'n Seeker expects a lecture after winning the game. I should'a snuck up the back."

Gretchen snickers.

Malcolm scowls.

Randy pishes.

"Randall," Malcolm begins again, "you did good last night, but we need to talk about your future."

Randy gets up and takes a pace or two around the room. "There are some serious flashbacks of the parental variety happening here. If it's all the same to you, could you just growl at me like you normally do and stop channeling Judge Parker?"

Malcolm eyes his snickering wife, "Quiet, Woman." He addresses Randy again, "RFI wants your help with an investigation. It could be dangerous work."

Randy waits. He gets nothing for his patience. "That's it? That's the lecture? Pish, that was nothing. Have to say, Mr. Mayor, you're not too good in the lecture department. You've time to practice, but I'm thinking DelRae is gonna rule this roost."

Gretchen laughs.

Gretchen pees a bit.

Gretchen scurries away—as quickly as an eight-month pregnant woman can scurry, that is.

Philly

Fred, Manuel, and Ted made great strides in recording and uploading Abigail Forrester's files. Their efforts slowed to a halt in the wee hours. The RFI guys camped out on the floor of the murdered woman's condo, the Philly guy headed to his empty house in Drexel Hill.

Detective Theodore Brothers is a 37-year-old man of color with close-cropped black hair, light green eyes, a perpetual five-o'clock-shadow, and a wide, toothy smile. He's 6'2" tall and built of solid muscle—the kind you get from playing sports and pounding the pavement—not the kind you get from bulking up at a gym.

On the two occasions Detective Brothers met with Detectives Serpico and Xavier, he was wearing his customary jeans, button-down shirt opened at the neck, and sport jacket. The most noticeable thing Ted Brothers wears is a simple gold wedding band that he touches often with his left thumb. When the Philly detective noticed the RFI guys eyeing the habit, he explained what he usually keeps to himself. "My wife, Janelle, was gunned down three years ago in a mall shooting. I wear the ring as a reminder of how quickly things go to shit." The conversation ended, there—the widower's thoughts, well not so much.

Just before noon, FICA Director Stacy Remington, knocks on a seemingly ordinary condo door. She immediately tucks her frosty digits into her coat pockets seeking warmth she knows she will not find. The stress she's been carrying from recent events has left her chilled to the bone and verbally fatigued. When she steps inside the condo, she raises a hand and shakes her head. The men get the message and busy themselves as she moves about scanning the layout and putting everything to memory. After a few minutes, she addresses the detectives, "I'm here to relieve you of your duties, gentlemen. I trust I will find everything in order."

"Yes, Director, if you'll follow me," Manuel says as he leads them upstairs.

At the top landing, the FICA director hands the RFI detective a summary she prepared on the organizational structure of The Realm. "Some work I've been doing, **from home**." She eyes him a beat too long, then gives him time to read the information. She uses that time to do a cursory tour of the murder scene and the home office.

One floor below, Fred is doing a once over in the kitchen. He runs the bagged up pizza boxes and beer bottles out to the car and is just about back inside when there's a knock and a walk-in at the front door. Ted Brothers extends his hand to the RFI detective, and offers a nod of the head and a "Ma'am," to the director who's making her way back downstairs. Within a matter of minutes, the law enforcement professionals lock up and leave the murder scene of Abigail Forrester. Stacy Remington ends her time with Manuel and Fred and follows Ted Brothers to the Granger Mitchell Carriage House on Old Estate Road. After a walkthrough, she releases the Celia Brettenvue murder scene to the PPD detective.

Manuel waits until Fred gets them on the highway toward Lewisburg. "The director prepared an organizational summary on The Realm. She gave me a copy for analysis. I think it has legs," Manuel smirks. "That statement is going to make a lot of sense to you when you see the summary. I'm pulling Researcher Randy in on this investigation."

"So much for making sense of shit," Fred quips.

Manuel laughs as he places a call and puts it on speaker.

Randy answers the blocked number, "Yo."

"It's Manuel Xavier."

"Agent 86," Randy whispers.

"This isn't a 1960s television spy show," Manuel snaps. "And if it were, we'd be from *Mission: Impossible*, not *Get Smart*."

"Sorry about that, Chief. So, what's the mission?"

"Fair warning. This KAOS shit will not be tolerated by Rocco Fiancetti, so know your audience."

The Kid laughs, "Appreciate your playing along, Mr. Smart."

Manuel addresses Fred, "It's been two minutes, and I'm exhausted."

"Warned you," Fred laughs.

Randy interrupts. "I'm guessing you called for a reason?"

"I want you to research the octopus, as in the sea creature."

"Rather watch 007 tangle with Octopussy, Mr. Xavier."

"Oh, for fuck's sake," Manuel hangs up.

"So much for making sense of shit," Fred repeats his earlier quip.

Is this a trick question?

Fred and Manuel let themselves into 275 Market Street and are rewarded with a squeal by the lady of the manor. “I’ll need a hoist and a hug from you both.” Once on steady legs, Gretchen hip-chucks Manuel. “I heard you were dismissed by Stacy from the Pennsylvania serial killer case. Did you have enough time to get a lead on who killed Abigail Forrester—or as Randy calls her—the redheaded frizzball nemesis?”

Manuel shrugs, “What we got was a heads up to document and preserve. What we do with what we got remains to be seen.”

Fred’s ears perk at the sounds of buzz saws and hammers coming from the game room, “I’m gonna check out the construction project.”

Gretchen calls after him, “It’s nice seeing you too, Fred.”

“Yeah. Yeah.”

Gretchen leads Manuel to the kitchen and hands him a letter, “That arrived for you.” He takes a seat at the table, she pulls stuff to make his favorite PB&J sandwich, light on the PB and heavy on the J. She talks to him over her shoulder, “I’m very sorry about Dominique.”

“Yeah.”

“Do you need to talk about it?” Gretchen offers a sympathetic ear knowing full well that Manuel’s feelings about Dominique are very complicated and offer little more than a deep source of pain.

He accepts his plated sandwich with one hand, takes hold of her wrist with the other, “When I do, you’re the first place I’m coming.”

She smiles and changes the subject, "Did you hear what happened at my father's law firm last night?"

Fred enters the kitchen interrupting the moment. “That looks good,” he nods toward the sandwich.

Gretchen gets up to make him one, “How do you like your PB&J, Fred?”

“Is this a trick question? I like it with PB and J.”

“How on earth does Kitt tolerate you?” she moans.

“She sends me here,” he laughs big.

Gretchen hands him his sandwich, “I was about to tell a story about The Kid. It sort of has something to do with the case you guys are, or were, working. My father was concerned about the safety of the Dominique and Celia Brettenvue files given the recent murderous events, so he asked Researcher Randy to go to his law firm last night to document and preserve legal memoranda and handwritten notes from meetings he and his colleague had with the now deceased women.

"In the dead of night, Randy was holed up in a photocopy room, just outside Daddy's office, when he heard footsteps approaching. He waited until the intruders went past his hiding place, then gathered his computer and files and snuck out. The guys heard Randy and started after him. The Kid pulled the fire alarm and jumped into an elevator just as the gun-waving men moved toward him. Fortunately, the elevator door closed and the would-be-file-absconders hightailed it away."

Manuel and Fred share a look, then Manuel offers some unsolicited advice, "Gretchen, you know there is some hinky shit with these murders. And now that the investigations have been redirected back down the chain—hinky doesn't even cut it. There could be valid reasons for the director of the FBI to move this investigation, but we don't have a clue about what's going on—and that leaves us scrambling."

"What Manuel is saying is that you need to stay out of this one," Fred counsels.

Gretchen nods. "Gentlemen, I am not going to do anything more than sit on that couch, flip through magazines and choose pretty things for DelRae's nursery. Now, you should know that while I sit—I think. While I think—I speculate. And when I have something to add, I will be doing so. I do love you for trying to protect me from myself, but I think you've met my husband. He's my first round of protection and by that I mean he acts like a prison guard. Oh, wait a minute, he was a prison guard." Gretchen rolls her cornflower blues. "Go, figure."

Manuel and Fred laugh at the beautiful earth momma, who reaches across and takes half of Fred's PB&J sandwich.

Mayor Price arrives home from the Borough Office a little after 8 PM and finds his woman fast asleep on the couch. After a few seconds with the sight of her, he brushes her short hair off her forehead and fingers a few strands. "Love this," he whispers.

Gretchen's smile spreads before her eyes open. "I must have dozed off," she yawns. "You missed Manuel and Fred, but they'll be by again tomorrow. They want to meet with you and Damian."

Well, that backfired.

Detective Ted Brothers works the Abigail and Celia cases **his** way—at his home office far from prying eyes—which is the way he likes things. The unconventional investigator uploads a computerized Venn diagram to help analyze similarities between the victims, the evidence, and the methods of murder. He starts filling the Venn. "Before I get too far in, let's put Dominique's information in. She's not my case, but she's relevant," he mumbles. With that addition, the Venn diagram has three overlapping closed curves creating a closed center curve. He puts information about each murdered woman in the appropriately designated outside sections, and notes, "Several logical relations."

He assigns an alphabetical letter to each victim: A-Abigail, C-Celia, D-Dominique, and begins running the Venn out loud. "A-C-D had personal relationships with Benton Brettenvue. A-C-D had associations with Antonio Alvarez. A-C-D were murdered inside locked or guarded locations. A-C most likely killed by lone individual. Access to D required multiple individuals. A-C-D died of asphyxiation, A-C were strangled, D died by poison that caused airway constriction.""

Ted takes a minute to analyze the Venn. "Just outside the center curve are variables that isolate certain parings between certain women: C-D were working with lawyers from Mitchell and Morgan. C-D have knowledge about Tango. C-D were on a 'hit list' issued by Antonio Alvarez, for varying lengths of times and for different reasons. A-D had associations with Malcolm Price and Gretchen Mitchell. A-C recently ended sexual relationships with Benton Brettenvue."

The analyzing detective repeats something he's already noted: "C-D were in guarded locations at the time of their deaths—C was under guard by Federal agents, D was in solitary confinement at a Federal penitentiary. A was behind locked and secured doors. All of the murders were very ambitious undertakings." He works for several more hours on the Venn, finishing up by making a list of questions. He is heading upstairs when he receives a call from Oscar Landry, a young officer at the PPD.

"Sorry to bother you at home, Detective, but we have orders to contact you with anything that might involve either of the murdered women."

"What have you got, Landry?"

"There's a log entry about a fire alarm going off at the Law Offices of Mitchell and Morgan the other night."

"Mitchell and Morgan, that's the firm representing Celia Brettenvue."

"Yes, sir."

"What were the circumstances for the alarm?"

"Someone inside the executive suite pulled the alarm shortly after 0100 hours. Philly FD recorded it as a false alarm, but…"

"Someone **pulled** that alarm," the detective finishes the officer's sentence.

"Yes, sir."

"Thanks for the information, Landry. Fax me the log page."

"Yes, sir."

The detective's mind didn't wind down until **late, very late**. His morning wakeup call comes **early, very early**, and in the form of a text request from Fred Serpico. "Do you have time for a meeting, tonight?"

"Yes."

275 Market Street
Fred and Manuel meet Ted Brothers in the underground garage and ride the privacy elevator to the top floor. The RFI team members expect a surprised reaction from the Philly detective when he realizes he's in the home of the legendary point guard, Malcolm Price. They are the ones who are left surprised.

Ted approaches with his hand extended, "77, it's a pleasure. You probably don't remember wiping the floor with me…"

"Ted Brothers," Malcolm smiles wide. "I'll be damned. I may have wiped the floor with you, but not until you drenched it with my sweat. Guys, this boy almost ended my high school winning streak senior year. We battled it out for State Champs in 1999. No one guarded me better then, or even in the pros." Malcolm fist pumps Ted and slaps him on the shoulder, "Good to know you're on board with these two clowns. Maybe now we can make sense out of this shit show. Come on, I'll introduce you to my wife, Gretchen, and the others. You probably know Jet Johnson, he's here as Captain of the Lewisburg PD."

"Well, **that** backfired," Fred laughs.

Introductions and reintroductions are made all around as everyone gathers in the new entertainment-game room, the most finished room of the current renovations.

Fred and Manuel wait while everyone finds a space. The wait is extended as Randy and Damian play rock, paper, scissors for the carnival-ride recliner. Randy wins—his enthusiasm is immediately quashed when Malcolm demands the recliner's buttons remain untouched during the meeting.

Damian laughs at his chair nemesis.

Malcolm shakes his head at the juvenile display.

Gretchen laughs at her husband's dismay.

Manuel pushes in—he is immediately interrupted by Randy, who addresses the group, "When Colonel Mustard and Professor Plum wrap up their game of Clue, I have a surprise lecturer coming in, so don't go roaming Boddy Mansion until you get the thumbs up from The Kid. Remember to thank me later."

Gretchen cracks up.

Damian rolls his eyes.

Malcolm growls.

Ted observes.

Fred and Manuel wonder. *The Body. Mr. Boddy.*

Manuel begins for real this time, "We have three dead women. They are connected to one another for a variety of reasons. Each of them has a level of notoriety for a variety of reasons. Their deaths are sensationalized news stories, and the public is eager to know what happened. Each of them is part of an investigation headed by FICA Director Stacy Remington. RFI was hired by Remington to work the Forrester homicide and to give an assist with the Celia Brettenvue homicide. The involvement of RFI has been terminated. From an investigative standpoint, our removal makes no sense, particularly since RFI has a 100% solve rate. We were a good hire by Remington and a bad fire by the FBI.

Just before noon, FICA Director Stacy Remington, knocked on the Forrester condo door. When she stepped inside, she moved about scanning the layout and putting everything to memory. After a few minutes, she addressed the detectives, "I'm here to relieve you of your duties, gentlemen. I trust I will find everything in order."

"Yes, Director, if you'll follow me," Manuel said as he led them upstairs.

At the top landing, the FICA director handed the RFI detective the summary she prepared on the organizational structure of The Realm. "Some work I've been doing, **from home**." She eyed him a beat too long, then gave him time to read the information. She used that time to do a cursory tour of the bedroom murder scene and the home office.

Then Manuel replays an earlier conversation he had with Fred…

"Gretchen gave this envelope to me when we first arrived."

Fred reads. Fred comments. "It's the same Octopus summary Remington gave you at the condo."

"Yeah."

"The director made damned sure you'd get your hands on **that** summary."

"Yeah."

"The Forrester and Brettenvue investigations have not been reassigned internally at the FBI. Rather, they have been kicked down to the Philadelphia police department and given to a seasoned, but overworked, detective. RFI is going to work these cases on the down-low. As we work through, we are going to bang up against a shitload of questions. Right now, the major question is why RFI was discharged from this case? I'm sure many of you share my gut reaction—that there are nefarious motivations involved—but we are investigators. We aren't going to rely on our gut reactions. The stakes are way too high. And since the stakes are high, everyone in this room needs to think twice before working this case. There are personal and professional risks inherent with this one. Once you are in—you need to stay in—so please be as sure as you can be before deciding."

He waits a beat-or-two-or-three. While he waits he watches as heads begin nodding their assent. Manuel continues, "There are three other people who will be working this case with us. Granger and Faye Mitchell and McKay Wallace. The three of them are going to provide assistance as needed. As for RFI, they will be our primary resource, **but** Stacy Remington was directed to get Rocco Fiancetti Incorporated off these cases. We need to have her back on this.

There can be **nothing** we do that leads our rogue investigation back to Stacy."

Randy interrupts again, "Just so you know, your head count is one shy. The Lecturer, who will be joining us shortly, will be part of this game of Clue. Trust me."

Eyes roll.

Randy laughs.

Fred takes over from Manuel. He hands out a sheet of paper, "This is a copy of a list made by Abigail Forrester. When Detective Brothers saw the names on the list, he kicked the case up the chain. When it landed on Stacy Remington's desk, she hired RFI. Let's review the list briefly. **Senator Turner Rodgers**: He is currently running as a Republican in the 2020 Presidential primary election. It looks as though he recently hired Abigail Forrester as his campaign manager, ending a nearly twenty-year estrangement between the two. **Benton Brettenvue**: He is an uncharged fugitive wanted in connection with the Tango investigation, as well as his association with Antonio Alvarez, and perhaps the recent deaths of his wife and mistress. **Topher Griffin**: He is the failed mayoral opponent of Malcolm Price. He is known to have been working with Abigail on instituting a fracking-inspired rape-and-pillage of The Keystone State. **Penny Meehan**: She is the investigative tabloid reporter Abigail Forrester hired to dig up dirt on Malcolm—first, about his relationship with Sage Finley, then on his mother Bertha King Price. For some reason Abigail put Penny's name on the list, then crossed it off the list. We are putting it back on. **Jack Cane**: He is the former Mayor of Lewisburg. He may have been pushed out of office so Abigail could get her candidate of choice, Topher Griffin, installed. If so, we will need to know what leverage Abigail used to accomplish that goal. **Senator Curtis Morgan**: He is the father of Malcolm Price. Both men have been targets of Abigail Forrester; we need to find out why that is. Since Senator Morgan is running for president, this part of the investigation is of paramount importance."

Malcolm balls his list and tosses it across the room.

Fred goes on, "The list is significant because it either identifies individuals whom Abigail Forrester was afraid of, or it identifies individuals who should have been afraid of Abigail Forrester. Manuel and I find it interesting that Malcolm's name is omitted from the list given Abigail's animus toward him. Perhaps, that omission will be explained as we move deeper into this investigation. We are divvying up assignments this way: Captain Johnson has agreed to work with me on the Lewisburg names, Topher Griffin, Penny Meehan, and Jack Cane. Each one of them were pissed at

Abigail; maybe one of them was pissed enough to kill her. I'll ride shotgun when the captain begins his questioning. Manuel and Researcher Randy will work on Senators Turner Rodgers and Curtis Morgan."

Fred addresses Malcolm, "You should give your father a heads up that we're going to be looking at him. Our gut says Abigail had a long game planned for Senator Morgan. If she was going to be working on Rodgers' presidential campaign, then she would have been banging up against Rodgers' opponent. That may be the totality of why Senator Morgan's name is on the list, but as far as Ms. Forrester is concerned, I don't think it's gonna be that easy."

Malcolm nods then shakes his head.

Manuel finishes off the meeting, "Granger Mitchell and McKay Wallace will be providing assessment on Benton, Celia, and Dominique Brettenvue based on information from their case files. Cyber diving will be done by Randy. I will be working with him and will try to keep him on this side of hacker's prison."

Randy interrupts again, "Pish, Manny, didn't know you cared."

"Call me Manny again and you won't live long enough to commit any cybercrimes."

"Noted, Colonel Mustard."

Manuel ends with a growl and living arrangement update, "Fred is going to be a houseguest of Captain Johnson during the investigations of Griffin, Meehan, and Cane. Then he will move in with Detective Brothers while they work the murder investigations. I am going to be staying and working at 275. If the renovations interfere with our cyber work, or we interfere with Malcolm and Gretchen, then we will work out of Mitchell and Morgan and stay at Granger Mitchell's place. I know this is a lot to digest, so why don't we break for Randy's surprise and talk again later."

The Kid pops from the recliner. "Stay where you are. I have a couple of things to deal with in the living room. Give me five, then come on in." Without looking back he calls over his shoulder, "Yeah, yeah, consider those eyes you're rolling as my chuck of the finger later."

Gretchen is the only one laughing.

Tango

The living room has been rearranged by the time the team enters. All of the furniture has been moved to the outer walls leaving a wide open space in the middle of the room. Gretchen takes a perch on the leather couch that now faces away from the windows and toward the living room. The men take seats. Malcolm takes his customary lean against the wall.

Smiles find the faces of those who know Peyton Wells, aka The Justice, when she steps in from the kitchen. She moves gracefully across the room and stands next to her partner. Peyton's 5'8" frame, dark asymmetrically cut hair, and Betty Boop face are in stark contrast to Randy's 6' frame, long, surfer-blonde locks, and meticulously cared for scruff on his youthful face.

She is hipster chic.

He is hipster cool.

They are hipster adorable.

Randy is in full control of the room as he addresses his audience, "Earlier, Mr. Xavier extended an invitation for me to participate in a little spy adventure."

"I hired you to do a job," Manuel growls.

"He gave me a research project. I smoked that research project with the aid of my banging hot assistant. These are our findings."

Manuel, Fred, and Malcolm growl.

Gretchen snickers.

Damian and Ted stay out of it.

Randy dims the lights; Peyton turns on the music. They meet at the center of the living room floor. Randy places a hand across Peyton's upper back, pulls her chest to chest and cheek to cheek, and they clasp hands on their outstretched arms. After a few upper body rotations, Randy begins leading Peyton. A few steps into the dance, she begins explaining their moves to their audience. "We begin with the canyengue Tango. The dance originated in the early 1800s along the Rio de la Plata between Argentina and Uruguay."

Randy moves Peyton across the floor.

"As you can see, my partner and I share one axis and dance in a closed embrace. Our legs are relaxed, wrapping and intertwining loosely, our direction dominated by the firmly placed leading and walking steps dictated by Randy. The canyengue Tango is very theatrical, powerful, and provocative." The dancers move across the floor for many intense seconds, he directs and she flourishes with an abundance of leg movements. Then they shift tone and stance for their next performance.

"We are moving into the nuevo Tango. You can see that Randy's embrace has loosened, accepting space between our upper carriages. This allows my partner to introduce variety and complexity into our footwork. The overall feel of nuevo is akin to improvisational jazz—it is best enjoyed when it is innovative and fresh."

Randy swiftly moves Peyton across the floor. There are no more words, only intense stares, dominance by him, obedience by her. They shift back and forth, between the dance styles, until Randy finishes their performance with dramatic flair. He pushes his partner down along his leg, his hand pressing her shoulder, her head coming to a rest on his outer thigh.

When the music dies, Gretchen breaks the heady silence that grips the room, "I think I am in desperate need of a cold shower. And if I smoked cigarettes, I'd be lighting one, possibly two right about now. That was hot!"

The men clap their agreement.

Peyton laughs.

Randy bows. "Before Mr. and Mrs. Mayor head to the shower to rinse, lather, and repeat, there is a quick lecture by The Justice," Randy bows again, "The floor is yours, babe."

"When The Kid told me about the armed file-absconders at Mitchell and Morgan and that the Legal Beagle..."

Gretchen interrupts Peyton, but addresses Randy, “Please, please, please, tell me you call Granger Mitchell, Legal Beagle to his face,” she all but explodes in anticipation.

“Damned straight, Mrs. Mayor.”

Gretchen cracks up laughing, “Gotta love The Kid.”

Malcolm shakes his head, “Whenever you two are finished...” He nods to Peyton to continue.

“Right. As I was saying, the Legal Beagle told Randy that RFI might be pulled from the ‘frizzy redhead’ and the ‘fantastic she’s made of plastic’ murder cases…”

Gretchen squeals in laughter, takes a look at Malcom and buries her face in her hands. Her shoulders shaking heartily.

Peyton rescues her friend from Malcolm’s imminent growl. “Anyway, when I was listening to the never-ending loop of news on TV about the recent murders, there was mention made of The Realm and the original eight members, and The Body, and Tango. The words left me with a nag. Then when Randy mentioned that Mr. Xavier asked him to research the octopus…”

Manuel and Fred growl.

Peyton jumps to her man’s defense, “Don’t worry, gentlemen, I can keep confidentialities.”

Manuel scoffs, “Good. Maybe you can teach him.”

Peyton laughs, "He's a secret keeper, but he's also a problem solver. This is how WE solved YOUR problem."

Gretchen snickers, buries her face, and snickers some more.

Peyton continues. "I know you are pressed for time, gentlemen, but I need to share this."

Her audience nods.

"Something one of my dance instructors said years ago began banging inside my head, so I did some research and found some interesting things. They may or may not have any direct correlation to the mysterious Tango case you are trying to figure out, but no stone unturned..."

Fred and Manuel nod and smile.

Peyton continues, "Like I said earlier, the Tango is a partner dance originated in the 1800s along the Rio de la Plata, an estuary between Argentina and Uruguay. The dance was born in port areas where natives mixed with slaves and immigrant populations. The original Tango is said to be a combination of the German waltz, Czech Polka, Polish Mazurka, Bohemian Schottische, Cuban Habañera, African Candombe, and the Argentinian Milonga.

"The Tango frame is called *abrazo*, or embrace. The closed embrace exhibited in our first dance is rigid, almost crushingly so. The open embrace exhibited in our second dance is flexible and adjusts to different steps. Both embraces allow the dancer's legs ample opportunity to intertwine and hook together in what is called the *Pulpo* which translates to The Octopus."

Peyton lets the information hang for a few seconds.

"An octopus has eight legs," Manuel says.

"Eight arms," Peyton smiles.

"An octopus has a body," Manuel says.

"A very interesting one," Peyton smiles.

Manuel eyes Fred who clearly wants in on the give and take, "Have at it, Fred."

"The Realm had eight leaders," Fred says.

"Eight arms," Peyton smiles.

"The Realm has The Body," Fred says.

"A very interesting one," Peyton smiles.

Fred smiles in return. "Peyton, what happens to the body of an octopus when it loses its arms?"

All eyes turn to the star of the evening.

"I thought you might ask, so I did a little research. The sea creature is a soft-bodied, eight-armed mollusk. Its mouth is at the center of the creature's arms. Its soft body can change rapidly and squeeze through the tiniest gaps. For the purposes of this analogy, all of those attributes are particularly beneficial. The Body of The Realm can change form, escape through tiny openings, and by nature, stay hidden while its arms thrash about gathering prey. Also of interest, for the purposes of this analogy, the octopus can replace severed arms. Perhaps, that's what The Body of The Realm is currently doing."

The room fades away.

Manuel pulls Stacy Remington's summary from his pocket for a read through; he hones in on the title.

<u>The Octopus</u>

<u>Organizational Structure</u>:
The Body.
8 ancillary leaders:
6 from South America,
1 from Africa,
1 from the U.S.

<u>Arrests</u>:
Antonio Alvarez: Peru
Binto Dube: Africa
Roland Gaffney: United States
Castro López: Argentina
Julio Romero: Chile
Raphael Ruiz: Brazil
Stiles Sigüenza: Guatemala
Migel Sosa: Columbia
*** Dominique Brettenvue:**
United States (potential replacement leader)
*** Dan Shea:**
United States (ancillary member)

Then Manuel replays his earlier encounter with Stacy at the Forrester condo...

"Let's table this discussion until after the meeting. Maybe Randy has something interesting on the octopus research project."

Manuel replays Stacy's words, again. This time, The. Penny. Drops. "The director was working on The Realm **from home**. Why?"

Fred is processing some shit at the corner to corner windows facing Hufnagle Park. Manuel joins him there. "Not sure what's banging through your head, partner, but I've got something. I don't think I mentioned that the director created The Octopus summary while she was in her **home office**. She made a point to let me know that – sorry to say I missed the significance of her statement until a minute ago. Stacy Remington has been working on the down-low and away from watchful eyes at the Bureau."

Fred nods. "Let me run what I've been thinking. I'll add that last tidbit about Remington working from home at the end. The director of FICA, with the approval of the director of the FBI, summoned you and me to J. Edgar for a meeting. While there, Remington gave us the murder case of Abigail Forrester. She began our meeting with these words: **I don't think The Realm is dead. The FBI, FICA, and RFI will be working that problem in coming days and weeks.** After that bombshell we were sent to Philly to take the

Forrester case away from the PPD because the murder victim had a list of names in her house that included some influential political figures. Rightfully, the decision was made that the Abigail Forrester case was out of the PPD's investigative league.

"Meanwhile, Celia Brettenvue, a federal prosecution witness under guard at a Carriage House owned by her lawyer was murdered—in the **same** way Abigail Forrester met her demise. You and I got a call from Remington dispatching us from one crime scene to the other. While at the second crime scene Remington discussed elements of the case with us as though we were part of, or would be part of, Celia Brettenvue's murder investigation. A day later, you and I were told—**on the QT** by Remington—that we were going to be removed from the Forrester investigation, and the investigation would be kicked back down the chain to the PPD, who originally had the case until it was deemed they weren't able to handle it. We were given that heads up **before** we were removed from the investigation, and we were also told to document as much stuff as possible.

"When the director arrived and did a walkthrough of the Forrester crime scene, she handed you a summary about The Realm, an organization we all believed RFI had decimated. Circle back to what Remington said during our meeting at J. Edgar: **I don't think The Realm is**

dead. The FBI, FICA, and RFI will be working that problem in coming days and weeks. Now throw in all the stuff Peyton said about The Body of The Octopus being able to regenerate arms or legs or whatever, and we end up with a whole lot of questions. The most important ones are: Why did the person who invited us to the party uninvite us? Why is she slipping us secret summaries that she's preparing at her home office? Why is she not working The Realm case at the Federal Bureau of Investigations, where she works at the highest security level with the type of resources required of this type of investigation?"

"Because someone inside J. Edgar has eyes on Director Remington."

Bodies, brogues, and beavers.

The Body is at his DC home. He is seated on a gray Queen Anne, wing-back, leather chair set near a crackling fire. A poured, but not yet sipped, Woodwind Reserve bourbon rests on a nearby table. The man's legs are stretched out on a thickly padded ottoman, his hands clasped and resting on his chest, and his two thumbs tap together in a sequential beat: *tap, tap, tap, pause, tap, tap, tap, pause*.

The contemplative figure in the quiet, dark room is taking stock, "Abigail Forrester, dead—Celia Brettenvue, dead—Dominique Brettenvue, dead. Three turncoats have been silenced. Individually, each could have inflicted structural damage. As a unified group, they could have brought the whole organization to its knees."

The head of The Realm is pulled from his thoughts by the muffled sound of a closing door. He gets up, takes his bourbon with, and goes to listen in.

Chevy Chase
Paul Ferraro is in his stately blonde brick home reading every major online newspaper from the Commonwealth of Pennsylvania. His interest in the Keystone State is limited in scope. "There it is," he says when he finds her obituary in The

Scranton Times-Tribune, "Ms. Forrester will be laid to rest at Pittston Avenue Cemetery…" He keys the address into his cell and continues scanning. He eventually finds what he next wants to know in the Philadelphia Herald, "The Philly PD is in charge of the Abigail Forrester and Celia Brettenvue murders. No FBI involvement? No RFI involvement? No fucking way!" He keys a note into his cell to check that shit out and continues scanning the newspaper. "Now let's see if there's anything on the breaking and entering at the law offices of Mitchell and Morgan…"

Boston is pulled from his work by the sounds of his family returning home. He runs downstairs, arriving just as his troops begin storming the kitchen. He moves backward in exaggerated form, absorbing the rush of little bodies and flying limbs, and their singsong, "Daddy's home!"

"Let's see how many there are today: one, two, three, four." Boston touches each child's head, smiles at his kids, then heads to his wife, Felicity, who's bringing up the rear. "Hey, babe," he smiles wide. "I've missed the hell out of you. Let's get the troops to bed early and do a little dancing."

The wife's smile dazzles at her husband's suggestion—after all, dancing is their code for sexual ravaging. "You know I love to dance, Paul.

Should I be warming up for any particular sway this evening?" she asks in her lilting brogue.

His smile cuts long, deep dimples as he runs his hooded lustful eyes over his mahogany-haired, blue-eyed, fair-skinned, Irish lass. "The Tango, of course."

The Realm Associate known as "Irish" nods and smiles at her man, "There's no dance quite like the Tango."

Beaver Falls

Benton Brettenvue is tiring of his no-tell-motel vacation. He's decided he needs a hobby and a pussy. Not necessarily in that order. Days of facial hair growth, sunning himself in the cold November air, and a ball cap pulled low, gives the fugitive enough cover to venture into town for provisions. After loading up on sandwich fixings, bottled waters, and bottled booze, he drops nearly $400 on outdoor clothing, hiking boots, and a fully outfitted survival backpack. Without question, the **best** thing Benton Brettenvue, aka Benny Terrio, picks up at Osterman's Outdoorsman is thirty-three-year-old Layne Osterman, a banging hot babe just back from a three-month trek across Alaska. The raven-haired, golden-eyed, bronze-skinned, survivalist-trainer agrees to give Benny private lessons in the great outdoors. Then, she agrees to give him private lessons in the great indoors.

Homicidal fantasies and ridiculous alibis. Part 1

Captain Damian Johnson and Fred Serpico arrive unannounced at Topher Griffin's house. They find him hammering a *For Sale by Owner* sign into his frost covered front lawn. He shimmies the sign a bit in the hole to make sure it's secured enough, tucks a rubber-tipped mallet under one arm, and removes a very scuffed leather glove from the hand he offers in greeting to the police captain. "I figured you would have come by weeks ago, Damian."

"Why's that, Topher?"

"Just assumed you'd start talking to the most recent person who wanted Abigail dead. As the days passed, it dawned on me that the list of people wanting that bitch dead would be a long one. I knew you'd get here eventually." Topher nods his head in Fred's direction, "Who's your friend?"

"Fred Serpico, with RFI," the captain offers.

"The guy who busted The Realm? Damn good work, Fred. Are you working the witch's murder case?"

"I'm in town on RFI business that's stalled a bit. The captain is keeping me off the streets by letting me ride along."

"Since you're here, you might as well come in."

The detectives sit at the kitchen table while Topher puts on a pot of coffee. "Damian, I'll tell you straight. I'm pissed that someone beat me to the punch with Abigail. Can't say if I'm happier she's dead, or more pissed I didn't do it," he sneers. "The bitch talked a big game of making Malcolm Price unelectable and promised me she could get me in as mayor, and then governor. We had a plan to frack the hell out of Pennsylvania." Topher raises his hand, "Don't bother expressing your opinions about the industry—" He stops talking long enough to deliver the men their coffees. "Bottom line, my association with Abigail left me up to my eyeballs in debt and out on my political ass. No one in the fracking industry will take my calls. I don't know shit from Shinola about any other business. And I didn't get to kill Abigail Forrester." Topher raises his cup of coffee in a mock toast, "But at least the witch is dead."

Damian shakes his head, "Topher, where were you the night of Abigail's murder?"

"Here. Alone. Drunk. That isn't the only alibi I have, Damian. If I killed Abigail you would have found her with duct tape across her mouth, drenched in an accelerant, and torched by a book of matches that had my fingerprints all over it."

Fred raises an eyebrow at the duct tape part of Topher's offering since that part has been kept from the press. He wants more from Griffin, so the affable detective plays along, "Sounds like you're saying that your alibi for the murder of Abigail Forrester is that the murder of Abigail Forrester didn't take place the way it would have taken place if you'd had the chance to murder Abigail Forrester," he laughs.

"That's exactly what I'm saying. Look, if fantasizing about killing Abigail could have made her dead, then I'm your guy. Then again there are probably hundreds who might have beaten me to the punch there, too."

"Have any names for the others who might have wanted Abigail dead?" Damian asks.

"Check the files in her filing cabinets. There are dozens of politicians across Pennsylvania and in DC who Abigail had the goods on. More locally, I'd say Penny Meehan and Jack Cane, maybe even Jack's wife, Monica. They all had plenty of reasons to want the witch dead." Topher snaps his fingers, "You know, Penny Meehan can back me up on my preferred method for killing Abigail. We discussed our fantasies one day at Hufnagle Park."

"And how did Ms. Meehan want to kill Abigail?" the men ask in unison.

Topher laughs, "Penny wanted to dig a deep hole, smack Abigail across the head with a shovel, push her in, and cover her with whatever dirt she dug up on her."

Damian shakes his head again, "Are you staying here until the house sells?"

Topher nods.

"Good. When it sells, or if your plans change and you need to leave these premises, you need to call me. Don't go **anywhere** without notifying me. Are we clear, Topher?"

"Very clear, Damian."

Homicidal fantasies and ridiculous alibis.
Part 2

Damian and Fred arrive unannounced at Penny Meehan's condo. Their knocks go unanswered and they are just about back to their car when an adjacent condo door opens. An elderly woman holding a fluffy white cat asks, "Are you looking for Penny?"

Damian approaches the septuagenarian, "Yes, ma'am. I'm Captain Damian Johnson with the Lewisburg PD."

The woman raises a hand and swats at the air, "I know who you are, Captain. I'm Mrs. Margaret Shanahan, and this is Popcorn," she holds her furry friend out in greeting.

Damian gives the feline a rub around the ears, "Any chance you or Popcorn know where I can find Ms. Meehan?"

"Is Penny in some sort of trouble?"

"Just following up on an investigation, ma'am. Someone mentioned she might be able to help."

"Because she's a reporter," Mrs. Shanahan surmises.

Damian nods.

"If you want to come back later, Penny usually gets in a little after 8 PM. If this can't wait you can find her at *Kiss and Tell*, the tabloid over on West. Can't say I approve of the tabloids, but Penny sure is a fine writer. Anything else, Captain?"

"No ma'am. Thank you for your help."

With that, Mrs. Margaret Shanahan closes her front door. In an instant a blue light from a television set fills the room to keep the lady and the kitty company.

The men wait outside *Kiss and Tell* hoping to catch Penny when she takes a break for lunch. They are leaning against Damian's car when an impossible-to-ignore woman exits the building. The long, lean, confident woman with black shorn hair and dark brown eyes gives the duo a once over. Her smile spreads wide as she moves in their direction.

Fred nudges Damian, "Penny Meehan is a GI Jane."

She smiles even wider at Fred's characterization. "Captain Johnson, I'm assuming you're here to see me?"

The captain nods, "Do you have a few minutes?"

Penny laughs, "It's going to take more than a few minutes to tell you how much I hated Abigail." She turns towards Fred, "You're Fred Serpico with RFI."

He smiles and nods, "That's right."

"I recognize you from the press reports on the Cappa Escobar and Micky Strong cases—

and The Realm bust, of course. It's nice to meet you, Fred."

They shake hands.

Damian steps back and lets Fred take point.

"Are you on your lunch break, Penny?"

"I'm heading across the street to Chip's. Tag along, gentlemen." The men follow the woman, who has absolutely no womanly sway, to a table for four in the back. They take her suggestion and order a corned beef on Rye with a cup of split-pea soup on the side. As soon as Chip delivers their food, Penny jumps in, "If I'd killed Abigail, she'd already be buried. I could have saved her family the bother of buying a plot in Scranton."

"We heard about your preferred method for killing Ms. Forrester," Fred smiles.

"Topher Griffin," Penny smiles and nods.

"He wasn't sending us to you as a suspect, he was suggesting that you didn't kill Abigail because her head wasn't bashed in with a shovel and her body wasn't buried beneath her own dirt."

Penny smiles, again, "Let me return the favor, using Topher's ironclad logic. Abigail wasn't killed by Topher because she wasn't gagged and torched, which is how Topher would have killed her."

Fred nods, "So, Penny why did you want Abigail Forrester dead?"

"Nice open-ended question, Fred. If this whole investigator thing doesn't pan out, come see me about a job in journalism."

They share a laugh before Penny gets serious. "I landed a job at *Liberty Rings* and was trying to go legit with my investigative reporting. Abigail approached me about digging into Malcolm Price's past, specifically his rumored relationship with Sage Finley, the sexual escort who was murdered near his ranch in Wyldwood, Texas. You know all that already. Anyway, Abigail convinced me to dig for dirt. She was gonna use the smut to quash Price's political aspirations, and I was gonna do a legit story about how the rich and famous sweep their dirt under pricey Persian rugs, with little or no push back from the cooperating cops." She smiles at Captain Johnson, "Present company excluded, of course."

"Of course," he nods.

"Anyway, seems there was a problem with our plan—a 6'5" problem. Malcolm Price figured out what Abigail was up to, and he pulled the rug out from under her. In an interesting and painful turn of events, I was the one flat on my ass after it'd been reamed by my editor. Months later, I took an incoming call from Abigail. This time she's pedaling a story that would supposedly make my career; she wanted me to dig dirt on Malcolm's mother and find out who his father is. She made a really compelling argument about

no one knowing who sired The Malcolm Price. There was **no way** I was passing on that story. So, like an idiot, I boarded the Abigail Forrester fucking train-to-nowhere." Penny stops talking long enough to take a bite of her sandwich, a slurp of soup, and a sip of soda, then pushes on.

"I researched the hell out of Bertha King Price. In the process I found a picture of her standing behind a young Curtis Morgan at the Forsythe fountain in Savannah from the early '80s. I called my editor, pitched the story, and he gave me the green light. *Liberty Rings* was ready to publish the Malcolm Price baby daddy story, but the Senator bested us by announcing his relationship with Bertha and his paternity of Malcolm at a press conference. That's the day I got fired. That's also the day the bitch got a job on Senator Turner Rodgers' presidential campaign."

Fred jumps in, "A *rumored job* on his campaign."

Penny shakes her head, "Nope. She had the job; it just hadn't been officially announced."

"How do you know she had it?" Fred asks.

"I went to DC and snooped around. I got it confirmed by several people."

"While you were there, did you dig up dirt on Abigail and Turner Rodgers?" Fred pushes.

"Yup."

"Is the dirt any good?"

"Yup."

"Care to share?"

"Meet me at my place tonight at 8. I'll show you what I have. There's one catch though, actually there are two."

Fred smiles, "There's always a catch with you journalism folks."

She smirks and shrugs, "Come hungry, I'm serving pizza. And I may need a comment or two, on the record, when the time is right."

Penny and Fred turn expectant eyes to Captain Damian Johnson, who nods his agreement, takes a bite of his sandwich, a slurp of soup, and a sip of soda to seal the deal.

Paydirt.

At exactly 8 PM, Penny leads her visitors through her open living-room-kitchen combo to a den-office combo down the hall. There are two large pizzas with a variety of toppings on each and a cooler of sodas and beers set on a table top.

"Help yourselves." Penny takes a bite of an already started pepper and pepperoni slice, chews a bit, and offers, "Let me finish this piece, then I'll talk while you eat."

The men plate their slices, Fred cracks open a beer, and Damian pops the top on a clear soda. The eager reporter puts the last bit of crust into her mouth, gets off her seat, pulls a covered banker's box from behind it, and lifts its top. She grabs a couple of files and puts them onto her lap.

"That box was empty a few weeks ago. Once I started digging for dirt on Abigail, it filled up quickly. I should give you a little background… I met Topher Griffin at Hufnagle Park the day after he quit the race. I told him I wanted to ruin Abigail and asked him to lead me to her dirt. He smiled and told me about a block tower Abigail had been building for twenty years—an **actual tower**—constructed of wooden blocks. The way Topher explained it,

Abigail dirtied up a politician, put his name on a block, and put the block onto the tower, then she moved the blocks around to help advance her goals."

Fred smiles wide.

"You've seen it—the wooden tower?" Penny accuses.

"No comment."

The woman chuckles, slaps her hand across her thigh, takes a sip of her beer, and continues, "Topher said if I really wanted dirt, I should concentrate on Turner Rodgers. He said Abigail told him she had the goods on the senator and that he was the first block she laid—take that anyway you'd like. As soon as Topher left Hufnagle, I got on the phone, got my old job back at the tabloid, got a retainer, and got my ass to DC. I already knew Abigail had interned for Rodgers, and after some research I learned that instead of her returning to Scranton when the semester in DC ended, she matriculated into graduate school. I'm pretty sure her three years at Georgetown were on Turner Rodgers' dime."

She eyes Fred.

He smiles wide.

"I'm starting to like you, Fred."

"Feeling's mutual, Penny."

"When I was done with the intern/grad student part of the story, I headed to the Library of Congress, where I hit paydirt. I found the roster for the Class of 1999 interns and plenty of pictures of young ladies and young men rubbing elbows with the Congressional leaders of our great republic. As it turned out, there were two interns in Congressman Rodgers' office in 1999: Abigail Forrester from Scranton and Kathleen 'Katie' O'Brien from Jessup."

Penny gets up, heads to the cooler, and grabs a couple beers and a soda. She hands them out on her way back, takes her seat, and picks up where she left off. "When I got back to Pennsylvania, I called Katie and told her I was doing a slasher piece on Abigail Forrester, to which she replied, 'Any chance you need a knife?' She damned near lost it when I told her that Abigail Forrester was slated to be named campaign manager for Turner Rodgers. Her first words were, 'What a stupid man to get tangled in her web, again.' Katie had a **lot** to say on the subject of Abigail Forrester, so we met at a little roadside diner, halfway between Lewisburg and Jessup. She held no punches when it came to the bitchy redhead. Katie said she and Abigail traveled to DC together and shared a room, but they never got close. She said Abigail never discussed the congressman in personal or professional terms, but it was very obvious the two were having sex in his office. Katie's impression was that it wasn't romantic or even friendly. She said Rodgers would call Abigail behind closed doors and within a matter of minutes she'd be back in the reception area, tucking in her shirt and putting her hair back into the clip she always wore."

Another stop. Another sip.

"Katie said when Abigail was in the outer office she spent her time rummaging through the congressman's personal files. Whatever real work the interns were supposed to be doing, Katie ended up doing it while Abigail did whatever the fuck she wanted. Toward the end of the internship, Katie said she started getting calls from Georgetown University asking that the congressman get in touch or send the documentation they requested. Katie said she couldn't testify in a court of law that Rodgers paid for Abigail's education, but she knows he did."

Penny gets up and grabs a slice of pizza while she waits for the men's' questions.

Damian goes first, "Where were you on the day Abigail Forrester was murdered?"

Penny shrugs her shoulders, "Not sure exactly. I was driving back from DC and got into Lewisburg after midnight."

"Did you make a side trip to Philadelphia, maybe swing by Abigail's condo?"

"Nope. I wanted to get back so I could meet with Katie. I **really** wanted to find out what happened between Abigail and the dirtbag running for president. If I hadn't been successful in DC, I might have taken the time to hit Philly and bash the bitch's head in, but the journalist in me was in charge, not the homicidal maniac," she smirks.

Penny hands one of the folders on her lap to Captain Johnson, "Those are copies of receipts from my trip to DC: gas station, hotel room and food receipts, and a handwritten record of what I did, where I went, and for the most part with whom I spoke. You can cross check the dates and times that I toured the Capitol; they keep a log of visitors. I only have copies because I attached the originals to my *Kiss and Tell* expense report."

Damian ignores the file and looks at Penny. "You have placed yourself within travel distance of Abigail Forrester's condo around the time of her murder, Penny," Captain Johnson explains.

Penny hands the captain a second folder, "Then I guess I'm at the mercy of you guys doing your jobs. Since I don't know the exact time of Abigail's murder, I can only give you my receipts to show you what I was doing that day and night—which was driving up from DC. The information in the second folder shows what I was doing over the next couple of days. There is a printout of an internet search I did on Katie O'Brien at 7 AM from the *Kiss and Tell* offices. There are cell phone logs showing my calls to her and travel receipts that document my trip to the diner where we met."

Penny waits while Captain Johnson scans the documents. She smiles when he pulls a printed copy of her rough draft hatchet job about Abigail from the folder. "I wrote that piece on Abigail when I got back from meeting with Katie. It's date and time stamped showing I worked on it the day **after** Abigail was killed, but before the news broke about her murder. Looking at this through the filter of a reporter, my questions would be: Would a killer continue chasing and writing a story about someone she wants to ruin, if she already killed her? Would an investigative reporter, one who is desperate for legitimacy, ruin her chances of breaking a story about the potential next president of the United States by killing the bitchy frizzy redhead who has all the dirt on him? I hope you conclude that the answer is no."

Fred chuckles, "So, your alibi for not murdering Abigail Forrester is that you wanted to ruin her in the press, gain legitimacy in the mainstream media, and get respectability from your peers, **before** you murdered Abigail Forrester."

Penny tosses her head back and laughs big, "Sounds ridiculous enough to be true—because it is, Fred."

As Penny walks the men to the front door she asks, "Will you two be at Abigail's funeral?"

"Are you going?" Fred asks. She shrugs her shoulders, "I might, but I'd place wagers that

Katie O'Brien will be there dancing on Abigail's grave," Penny smiles wide.

"Yeah? What grave dance do you suppose Katie O'Brien will be doing?" the RFI detective casually asks.

"She's an Irish lass, so I suspect she'll be doing a jig."

Whispered echo.

Manuel and Randy spend a good part of the morning converting the former campaign office at 275 to the Diving Center. Before Randy goes on his first RFI-sanctioned dive, Manuel sets the limits, “Keep it legal.”

“Pish, you’ll never know one way or the other, Mr. Xavier.”

“You’re that good?” Manuel challenges.

“I’d say, ‘you’ll see’, but you won’t.”

“In that case, I’m heading to the kitchen for a PB&J, need anything?”

“A PB&J sounds good.”

“Yeah, how do you like it?”

“Heavy on the PB and hold the J,” Randy laughs.

Manuel is shaking his head on his way through the construction landmine known as the future nursery of DelRae Price when he receives a call from the Decadent One aka Leavy.

“Miss me already?” Manuel teases. He stops when he hears what sounds like sobs coming from the other end. “Leavy? Leavy? What the hell? Words, Leavy, give me words.”

Through a catch in her voice she says the only name that could bring the seasoned professional to tears, “Dan Shea.”

Manuel waits through several unsettling seconds of near-silent sobs. “Leavy, give me more,” Manuel gently pushes.

“Dan Shea—you know, the son-of-a-bitch who kidnapped me and sold me to The Realm—was murdered in prison. Sorry for the emotions, Manuel, I guess the news just pushed my buttons.”

“It’s pushing mine too. What can I do to help?”

“You taking my call helped. I’m good now.”

“Leavy. You’re entitled to tears. Don’t ever hold them from me. We’re good. Right?”

“Right. Check your system, I’m sending the information on Shea. And Manuel, his death is way too timely. It feels like someone is cutting a bunch of loose ends. And Manuel…”

“Yeah, Leavy.”

“Shea's death is welcome news,” she whispers.

“Call me when you need me.” Manuel stays on the line long after Leavy disconnects, running her words…

…“his death is way too timely. It feels like someone is cutting a bunch of loose ends. And Manuel…”

His thoughts are held by the whispered echo of his name. He moves aimlessly through the penthouse ending his stroll at the bank of windows in the great room. The hustle on Market

Street and at Hufnagle Park should capture his attention—it doesn't. Manuel's headspace is locked by the events that brought Leavy into his life…

"You are safe, for now. Follow my directions explicitly. Do you understand, Agent?"

Leavy nodded.

Manuel removed Leavy's blindfold. He waited for her eyes to adjust to the morning light. Recognition flooded her face.

"You're FBI," she croaked.

"Yes."

"You're undercover in The Realm?"

"Until this morning, yes. Once they realize I have taken the cyber huntress, known as 2.0, they will realize my duplicity. I am a dead man if they catch me. You are a dead woman if they catch you. I suggest we work together to make sure they don't catch us."

~

The agents, one who had infiltrated a Peruvian crime syndicate, and one who had helped escaped sure-imprisonment there, entered a farmhouse root cellar a few minutes before midnight. He placed a call, said two words, "fiat lux," and disconnected.

She turned stunned eyes his way. "Who are you really? And how do you know about fiat lux?"

"I am FBI, or at least I was this morning. My father is MI6. You know him as Rocco Fiancetti," he smiled broadly and proudly.

"Oh. My. God." Leavy exclaimed.

He tossed his head back with a laugh. "No, he's not God, although he thinks he is."

"Rocco Fiancetti has a son, and you are that son?"

"Yes."

"So technically, Rocco Fiancetti has possession of DOA, the Girl Genius, and 2.0."

"Until I release you to Special Agent, John Maxwell, I have possession of 2.0."

~

At midnight John Maxwell received a text from Joy Fiancetti that read: **fiat lux, root cellar**. The Special Agent entered the dark, dank space and found Agent Hannah Leavy waiting. A man stepped from an alcove behind her. The men pulled handguns. The men each took hold of one of Leavy's hands and pulled.

She shook herself free. "For God's sakes, give me your guns. Now!" She put both weapons in the waistband of her sweats and squared-off at the men. "Listen up. I'm cold, hungry, and in desperate need of a shower. I've been in these running clothes for days and may have pissed my pants once or twice, so the three of us are going inside to talk. When we are done, I'm taking care of my girly needs." She moved away, then stopped cold. "And I am warning you both—don't ever hold my hand. Ever!" Leavy turned to John. "Manuel is FBI. He was undercover in The Realm and rescued me moments before I was put onto an LNG tanker headed to God knows where…"

"Peru," Manuel interrupted. "The tanker was headed to Peru. Antonio Alvarez is gonna be very pissed that 2.0 is not on that tanker."

Then Manuel remembers the things that keep Leavy from sharing his life…

"Dead On Assignment."

She waited for him to say more, he didn't. Leavy edged away from Manuel and repositioned the flashlight they shared. A beam of light found a portion of his face and illuminated it in a Blair Witch sort of way. "Am I to expect other words?"

"No."

"Very well," she moved back to her usual spot behind the paneled wall. "I wish we'd had time to hit the treadmill before the detectives stopped by."

"They stop by a lot."

"They're dedicated to finding me."

"They would have found you on Day One if Maxwell and the rest weren't circumventing their efforts. They're good."

"John said they are the best detectives he's worked with. Ooo. Ooo. Cramp." Leavy slid her back across the wall, lay flat, and put her leg onto Manuel's lap, "The calf. Crammmmp."

"Flex your foot. Pull it back as far as…"

"Ahhhhh. Yes, right there."

She moaned her release of pain. He got hard.

~

"Dead On Assignment."

"Am I to expect other words?"

"It's a lonely life."

Leavy shrugged and moved further away.

"You do that a lot … move away whenever this topic comes up."

"What topic, Manuel?"

"The one you refuse to discuss."

"Have you something to ask?"

"You haven't mentioned anyone, family or friends, or anyone really who might be wondering about you."

Leavy went from calm to panicked in a heartbeat. She started hyperventilating and clawing at her clothes. "I need to get out – of – here."

"Shhhhh. John isn't alone. Serpico and Phelps will hear you. Shhhhh."

Manuel watched helplessly as Leavy unraveled, as she pulled near everything off her body, as she broke, and as she struggled to pull herself back together.

"I need you to hold me. I don't want to talk about anything. I just need you to hold me."

He opened his arms to her. She nestled in. After several minutes…

"A tornado hit my family's home. I survived."

~

"This is our last night in the cave," Manuel nudged Leavy with his foot. Perched on either end of a leather oxblood couch set near a century-old fieldstone fireplace, the AWOL Federal agents readied themselves for their next adventure.

"It's happening at warp speed."

"We've been here for two months, Leavy."

"Yes, but within hours of John's leaving FICA, he and I are heading to a compound located who-knows-where, to live amongst a group of people hiding from who-knows-who, for who-knows-how long. Not exactly how I'd planned my life."

Manuel nudges her again, "You and John…"

Leavy waits through a lengthy pause, pushes in when there's nothing more from Manuel. "Have you something to say, or to ask?"

"Things will be different at The Compound. You will be sharing quarters with John … you'll be living together. The time you've spent with him so far has been … unconventional."

She laughed and agreed. "Unconventional covers it nicely."

"You've spent very little alone time with John."

"Yes."

"Are you planning a life with him?"

"You will be reuniting with Dominique and beginning your lives together—bringing a new life into the world. Things are set, are they not?"

"Yes."

Then Manuel admits a terrible truth—he brought another woman into his bed because he couldn't have Leavy…

Manuel arrived back at The Compound late from his trip to Lewisburg having been set straight on a few things by Mama Girl. He spent the night camped out on the couch, so as not to disturb Muriel and Charlotte. That. Is. Bullshit. He stayed on the couch because Mama Girl's words cut deep. They banged the shit out of him on the trip home and all through the night. They were still banging hard as he made his way across The Compound grounds…

"What's the truth about the woman who's sharing your bed, Manuel?"

He shook his head, "Muriel needs a place to stay. I need help with Charlotte. I guess you could say we're at a mutual place of needing each other."

"Sounds like an awful place to be."

Manuel is deep in thought when Fred exits the privacy elevator. The detective coughs as he walks toward his partner, coughs again to pull Manuel from his thoughts. He tries something else. "Manuel!"

The dazed man turns and blurts, "Dan Shea is dead."

Fred nods, "Your father called and told me, he asked that I check on you."

Manuel smiles, "Rocco Fiancetti is getting soft in his old age. I'm fine Fred, but Leavy's shaken up by all this."

"Rocco said she asked for a few days away from The Compound. She leaves tonight."

"Is John going with her?"

"Nope."

"Where is she going?"

Fred stares Manuel down, "I'm sure you'll figure that out for yourself."

Researcher Randy bounds into the living room just as the elevator door closes with Manuel behind it. The expression on Mr. Xavier's face suggests that PB&Js are no longer on the afternoon menu.

Fred addresses The Kid, "Do you know who Dan Shea is?"

Randy nods. "He kidnapped the Decadent One and tried to ship her to Peru. Why?"

"He's dead."

"Someone sure is busy snipping loose ends."

Fred nods, "Come on Kid, let's go pull some loose ends and see what unravels."

Manuel

Manuel won't call Leavy. "There's no need to discuss this." He shuts off his cell and tosses it onto the passenger seat. He turns on the radio and presses the scan button, pretending to listen to the first few seconds of a handful of songs. His head isn't into the music. Hell, it's barely into the drive up I-84E. "We've been on a collision course since we met," he admits. A Maverick Cross song disrupts his thoughts. He scoffs, "*Rain Down*." He stops the scan so it can play through, slams his hand hard on the steering wheel, "Fuck Leavy, this shit happens tonight, or it never happens." He settles in for the six-hour drive, a tortured, "Full circle," ending it all.

Leavy

Leavy won't call Manuel. "There's too much to discuss." She shuts off her cell and tosses it into her overnight bag. She puts in a set of earbuds and presses shuffle on her iPod—the only thing that survived the tornado. She listens to the first few seconds of a handful of songs—begging the music to take her out of her headspace. "There's something between us," she admits. A Maverick Cross song disrupts her thoughts. She scoffs, "*Rain Down*." She suffers through the lyrics only to get to the piano piece. His piece. "This happens tonight, Manuel, or I walk away." She settles in for the two-hour flight, a whispered, "Full circle," ending it all.

Full Circle

The woman who needs to move below the radar of the best spies in the world, discreetly flashes her RFI credentials to the rental car clerk, “I need to pay cash. There can’t be any information logged into your computer system.” The very young attendant gets totally hooked by the whole cloak and dagger thing going on and readily complies. Leavy repeats the process at a hotel located somewhere between Boston and Everett.

Within one minute of entering the hotel room, Leavy is stripped bare and in the shower, pressing tight against the cold tiles and lowering herself to the floor. She wraps her arms around her knees, drops her head onto them, and surrenders to the emotions she should have dealt with a year ago. Then she deals with the emotions that keep coming around and around—like the tornado that changed everything—that took everything.

“I fucking hate you! You took me. You sold me. You changed me.” Those screams and sobs are directed at Dan Shea. “I fucking needed you! You left me. Forever. You never said goodbye.” Those screams and sobs are directed at her parents. The shattered woman stays heaped on the floor of the shower for hours. As the last of her pain and suffering washes down the drain, she pulls herself upright, leaving the mists of misery and fragments of her life behind. She pulls her wet hair high, pats her wet eyes dry, drives to an abandoned printing plant parking lot, and waits for whatever lies ahead.

Manuel cuts the lights as he pulls into the parking lot where he first laid eyes on Leavy. He knew from the moment he touched her that he wanted her. He knows if he touches her tonight, he will do whatever it takes to make her his. A satisfying groan leaves him as he inches his car toward the lone one sitting at the far end of the parking lot under the only working light.

He parks and sits for a moment staring at Her. Soft illumination touches her here and there, but it matters little. Manuel knows every inch of Leavy. He knows the softness of her long, wavy mahogany hair, the playfulness of her pale green eyes, her beautiful full lips, the ones made for long, slow kisses. Kisses he aches for. He gets out and walks to the rental. He knuckle-wraps the driver's side window.

She startles awake and begins sobbing when she sees that He has come.

Manuel opens her door and offers her his hand. She grabs onto it and lets him pull her into his arms—the physical and emotional movements reminiscent of when he pulled her from the steel drum. That jolt of desire, from so long ago returns and is even more intense. Manuel closes her door and presses her back against it. He takes her face in his hands and holds it steady.

"Leavy. This thing we are about to do can't be a once only thing. If we aren't going to be together, really together, without others in our lives, then you need to tell me to leave." Manuel runs his thumbs over the tears that wet her cheeks. He wants to kiss her, taste her, touch her, enter her, but he can't be with her, then leave her and live without her.

"Manuel. There's something between us, there always has been. I know you should leave, but I can't be the one to tell you to. I just can't. Not anymore."

The wanting man presses the length of himself against her, she moans. He feels the rise and fall of her breasts against him, he groans. He kisses her cheek ..... the corner of her mouth ..... her lips. She quivers, then surrenders to the touch of his tongue on hers. Manuel relaxes against her. Leavy wraps her arms and holds on tight. They revel in the taste of their future—then he pulls away.

"Leavy, we're doing this, all of this—but we need to take care of the ones we're leaving behind."

She nods, "I need to talk to John."

"I'll come back to talk to Muriel in a day or so."

Leavy runs her fingers through his hair, "We're doing this."

"All of this."

He follows her to Logan and waits with her until her flight is called, then grabs a couple hours sleep at Leavy's hotel room. He begins his six-hour trip back to Lewisburg—daylight his only companion.

You whisper her name.

Fred leaves the Diving Center when he hears his partner enter the guest suite at 275. Given that Manuel was with Leavy the night before, the detective expected his friend would be unwound and happy—he figured wrong—the man he finds is twisted in knots and surly.

"What do you want, Fred?"

"What I **want** is to know what happened. What I'll **do** is prepare you for what's going to happen. Muriel is leaving The Compound tonight. She's heading back to Penobscot Bay to stay with Jackson Page at Pickering Farm. Tank is being sent with her and will stay on the Island until we know what response she gets from her fans. Kittridge is going to be taking care of Charlotte until the dust settles. You need to head to The Compound and deal with this mess, Manuel."

"Leavy and I aren't together, at least not in the way we want to be."

Fred shakes his head, "You're a dumbass if that's what you think. You and Leavy have always been together. I'm not making a judgment about what you and Leavy are doing, or are going to do, but you guys dropped a bomb on The Compound, and you need to go pull some shrapnel from the walking-wounded."

Manuel nods. "You said Muriel is leaving. What about John?"

"Ohhhhh .... he's staying put. He plans on beating the shit out of you when you get back. Consider this a heads up, you've got it coming from all sides. Rocco and Joy are staying neutral on the romantic issue, but from a professional standpoint they don't want to lose their best cyber defender, so there's that. Mike and Steve are keeping their opinions to themselves, but the women, not so much. Last night Kittridge said she and Maura always thought you should be with Leavy. Don't think for a minute that means they aren't pissed at you two for sneaking off and meeting up last night."

Manuel shakes his head, "It wasn't like that— We didn't plan anything. We just ended up at the same damned place."

"The LNG facility in Everett," Fred surmises.

"Yeah. We came clean about how we feel for each other and decided to put the two of us on hold until we have a chance to talk things out with John and Muriel." Manuel pauses and runs a thought, "If people at The Compound sensed there was something between Leavy and me, then John and Muriel must have known it, too. Leavy must have walked into a hornet's nest when she got back last night. I need to go back."

Fred smacks his friend on the shoulder, "The RFI jet is waiting for you at Fox Hollow. Grab your gear, I'll take you."

Halifax

Mike is waiting at the airport. He offers Manuel nothing by way of judgment, but gives him fair warning about John, "His pride is broken, and he plans on leaving you the same way."

Manuel nods.

Mike and Manuel are met by John and Steve on the driveway. Rocco is watching from the deck of the Main Cottage, his arms folded across his chest. The father and son catch eyes and acknowledge one another with a slight nod of the head.

John makes a move toward Manuel, but is blocked by Mike and Steve. "When your bodyguards aren't around, Manuel, we need to settle this."

Manuel nods. "After I deal with my **women,** you'll get your piece of me," Manuel turns and walks away leaving Mike and Steve to deal with a raging John.

Manuel starts toward the cottage he shares with Muriel; stops when he sees her standing at the edge of Roseway River. She turns and smiles when he nears, "Looks like the jig is up."

Manuel remembers those as the first words she ever said to him. He steps to her and pulls her into his arms, "I'm sorry, Muriel. I just can't pretend, anymore."

She steps out of his embrace, "I know. I've always known, Manuel. I don't blame you or Leavy. I appreciate that the two of you gave others a chance to capture your hearts." She pauses, not sure if she should say more .... "You know, you said her name once when we were making love, and you whisper it sometimes in your sleep."

A deep pain crosses Manuel's face. Muriel takes hold of his hands. "I'm not telling you this to cause you pain, Manuel. Our hearts feel what they feel, and they can't be forced to feel anything else." She squeezes his hand, "You should know that Leavy has moved out of John's place and he is beyond pissed. I think he wants his pound of flesh, though if he's honest with himself, he always knew how you two felt about one another."

Muriel steps toward Manuel. He opens his arms for her and she nestles in.

"Muriel, I…"

"Please don't Manuel. Just hold me for a minute, then let me go."

"Back to Pickering?"

"Yes. There is a gay septuagenarian eagerly waiting my return." She offers a wonderful smile to the man who saved her and helped her find her way back to who she is. "I should go say goodbye to Charlotte."

Manuel waits outside the Main Cottage while Muriel takes that moment with his daughter. He is still at the river when the transport vehicle leaves The Compound. After a few minutes he goes looking for his baby. He finds Charlotte in the Mahoney-Serpico suite. Kitt places her hand onto Manuel's cheek as she places his daughter into his arms. "Do you need an ear?"

"Not now, Kitt, but after my time with John..."

She sheepishly smiles, "I doubt you'll be able to talk much after he's done with you, Manuel. I've known John since we were kids, I've raised three children with him, we had a huge falling out and went our separate ways—even through all that, I have **never** seen him so pissed."

"Good to know, Kitt."

Manuel spends time with his child then leaves when Mike returns from the airport. The father who is scheduled for a beat down hands his baby girl to Kitt and heads outside. He calls out to Mike, "Tell John I'm waiting for him at the Athletic Center, and you better tell Maura to be ready at the Medical Center."

Sucker punched.

The men meet at center ring. There are no boxing gloves and no protective gear, just two men eager for fisticuffs action. Mike and Steve are the only other people in the gym. Mike is inside the ring with the men, "Keep it clean," he warns them, before stepping out.

Manuel snarls at John, "Take your best shot. I won't block the first punch because I deserve it, but know this, you won't land a..."

Before Manuel finishes his sentence, John delivers a blow to Manuel's left cheek. The taste of blood unleashes him. He takes several body punches from John, before letting loose a torrent of punches. They are quick. They are powerful. They bust up his opponent.

After several minutes, Mike and Steve jump into the ring and separate the men. The physical assault may be over, but the verbal assault is well under way. "I should have killed you when you first showed up at my place with Leavy. I knew you wanted her then, and I've lived with your wanting her ever since."

Manuel smirks, "What man tries to keep a woman who doesn't want him?"

John lunges at Manuel, "You son-of-a-bitch!" Mike and Steve wrangle him back.

Silence falls over the Athletic Center when Rocco Fiancetti speaks from the doorway, "**That** is enough. Choices have been made; fists have been thrown. Get medical attention and stay out of one another's way. Manuel, after your time at the Medical Center, see Leavy then go back to Pennsylvania. The jet will return you there tomorrow, so make your decisions with her tonight. John, decide what your future is and tell me in the morning. Mike and Steve, confiscate their weapons and don't let them near one another again."

With that, the two injured men are escorted to the Medical Center.

Maura moves between exam rooms thankful Mike and Steve are standing guard outside each. John bears the brunt of injuries; an x-ray reveals two broken fingers, most likely the result of the first punch thrown. He has a black swollen-shut eye, cut lip, and a cheek that needs stitches. While painful, his injuries will mend.

Manuel's left cheek is the only injury. "No break of your facial bones, but you have a nasty cut inside your mouth, and you should get your teeth looked at," Maura informs.

"The bastard sucker punched me."

"Yeah, well, you should have expected it."

"Yeah?"

"And John should have expected Leavy to leave him for you in a heartbeat."

Manuel locks eyes with Maura, "You knew that did you?"

She rolls her eyes and exhales big, "Some fucking detective **you** are. Well, things are settled now and people are where they're meant to be. Drama done."

Manuel smiles wide, then reacts from the pain of it.

Maura hands her patient a bottle of pain meds, "Take these and by that, I mean, t.a.k.e. t.h.e.s.e. Now, get out while I finish up with John."

Manuel hops off the exam table, stops when Maura touches his shoulder, "Leavy is waiting for you at your cottage."

Her whispered name.

Relief rolls off Leavy when Manuel comes bounding into the cottage. She is standing by the fireplace, its amber glow backlighting her beautifully. She doesn't move toward the man she wants; she waits for him to come to her, to claim her.

Manuel relaxes into the moment, into the thing that has had its hold over him. "Leavy," the sound of her name is different, resonant. He takes the room in two steps, wraps his arms and pulls her to him. He holds her. Just holds her, pulling in her scent, letting it settle deep. He relaxes their embrace, stares into her eyes a bit, and lovingly traces the contours of her face. He notices the tremble in his fingers and welcomes his total surrender to this woman—his woman. Manuel takes her face in his hands and says the words he's never said to another woman, "I'm in love with you."

Leavy smiles wide, gently puts her fingertips to Manuel's injured cheek, "I know." She places a feather-soft kiss to his lips. "Sure wish you didn't get these all busted up. I had plans for them."

"Come on. We'll figure something out."

The couple, the one who'd waited a very long time to be together, wait through a few more hours of gentle touches and words of promise. When he finally enters her, her satisfaction is immediate—his soon after— and it is announced with the whisper of her name, "Leavy."

Wheels and other things are up.

The lovers leave The Compound early the next morning without seeing anyone but Mike. Nothing is said between the travelers until the couple is ready to board the jet.

Mike offers his hand to Manuel, “You and John. That was some shit.”

Manuel smiles and winces, “Yeah.”

Mike pulls Leavy in for a long hug, “You and Manuel. That is some shit.”

Leavy smiles w.i.d.e. “Yeah.”

The newsome-twosome settle in as the jet taxis. Things they should have discussed the night before get said while high above the clouds, “We’re doing this?”

“All of this,” he takes her hand and kisses her knuckles.

“John needs to stay working at RFI,” Leavy begins.

“He will.”

“What makes you think so?”

“He’s pissed, but he’s John Fucking Maxwell, the best cyber defender in the world. He’s not gonna leave the best cyber intelligence agency in the world because his pride is wounded.”

She nods and looks out the tiny window. After a bit she begins again, “Do you think

Gretchen and Malcolm will mind my camping out with you for a bit?"

"No."

That's it. Nothing more is said. Nothing more needs to be said because He and She are together.

275

Realizing he hadn't asked permission from Mr. and Mrs. Mayor, Manuel takes Leavy to the guest suite via the back entrance. He leaves her there and goes in search of the unknowing landlords. He finds the pregnant half of the duo perched on the leather couch overlooking Hufnagle Park. He joins her there. She sort of rolls to his end of the couch and touches his swollen cheek, "I'm afraid to ask how John is if you look like this."

"He's alive," Manuel growls.

"And Leavy, how is she?"

"She's here."

"Good," Gretchen says with a sweet smile and a nod.

Manuel shakes his head in disbelief, "Are you going to tell me you knew we had feelings for one another?"

Gretchen laughs, "Of course. The question you should be asking is who didn't know about you and Leavy."

"How about 77, did he know, or is this just some sort of woman voodoo thing?"

Malcolm answers Manuel's question as he exits the privacy elevator, "77 knew." When the man gets close enough he asks, "How's the cheek?"

"It's been better."

"I heard you unleashed on John at bit."

"A bit," Manuel nods.

Gretchen twists on the couch and addresses her man, "Leavy is here, you know."

"Didn't know, Woman. Where's she at?"

Manuel gets off the couch and goes to get the woman in discussion. When they return they are met with warm embraces from the mister and misses of the mayoral manor. Nothing about the circumstances of Manuel and Leavy being together is discussed again that night. Not even when Fred Serpico joins the group for dinner. After two bites of food, Manuel tells Fred that Kitt wants him back at The Compound to help her with a project.

Fred pushes back from the table, "I've got to go. Damn, Manuel, why didn't you lead with that information?"

Leavy laughs at Fred knowing full well why Kitt wants him home.

Manuel gets up from the table and smacks Fred on the shoulder, "The jet is waiting at Fox Hollow. Come on, I'll take you."

There is no crew aboard the jet when Fred steps in. "Dammit. There's gonna be a delay."

He starts moving toward the back just as The Beatles tune *In My Life* fills the space around him. He laughs big, "Kittridge ……. are you on this jet?" He moves further down the aisle and finds Her, "Kittridge Anne Mahoney, what are you doing here?"

The beautiful woman with peaches and cream skin, warm, nutty brown hair and eyes, and a million-watt smile, goes all come-and-hithery, "I'm here to get you **off** the ground, Mr. Serpico."

The very eager man drops *trou*. The very eager woman squeals with delight.

"Fasten your seatbelt, Kittridge—I coming in for a landing."

The tarmac-twosome make quick work of their project. Twice. Just before it's wheels up, Kitt calls out to her departing man, "Thank you for flying Mahoney Airline. We hope you'll be boarding again, soon."

"Only airline I'll ever fly," he says on a laugh. Then calls over his shoulder, "I'm happy, Kittridge."

"Me, too, Fred."

Behind closed doors.

For the past several days, the director of the Federal Investigative Cyber Agency has been behind closed doors working a problem—a problem with 1 body and 8 appendages. It should be noted that the office doors Stacy Remington is behind are those of her home office. She abandoned J. Edgar when it became conclusive—in her mind—that she is under surveillance, "My movements, my calls, my files, my file requests, my cyber dives, my damned keystrokes, all of them are being monitored. Well they can't monitor my home system—it is impenetrable."

The determined director has been up for hours working feverishly at her secure system. At this particular moment however, she is stuck in neutral. She's reviewed The Realm summary she prepared and handed off to Manuel, umpteen times already. After each review she repeats the word she thinks is key to her investigation, "octopus." She counsels herself, cajoles herself, admonishes herself, "Work the damned problem!" She takes a walk around her office, stops at a window that overlooks her postage-stamp-size front yard, and ponders. She returns to her desk many minutes later and reads the summary one more time…

The Octopus

Organizational Structure:
The Body
8 ancillary leaders:
6 from South America,
1 from Africa,
1 from the U.S.

Arrests:
Antonio Alvarez: Peru
Binto Dube: Africa
Roland Gaffney: United States
Castro López: Argentina

Julio Romero: Chile
Raphael Ruiz: Brazil
Stiles Sigüenza: Guatemala
Migel Sosa: Columbia
*** Dominique Brettenvue:**
United States (potential replacement leader)
*** Dan Shea:**
United States (ancillary member)

And something shakes loose!

Pun intended.

Fred got back from his airport tryst with Kitt after his host and hostess had retired for the evening. He snuck into the Johnson guest room feeling much like a sixteen year old—a very unwound sixteen year old. He is up with the birds the next morning, and when he enters the eat-in-kitchen, he pulls the pint-sized Wanda into his arms and dances her across the kitchen floor. She cackles with delight, a sound Damian is most accustomed to hearing within the confines of their bedroom. When Fred dips Wanda low and places a kiss on her cheek, she pulls him up short, "You need to inform me before your woman comes to town, so I can protect myself from your morning ravages."

"And how do you know my woman was in town?"

"Manuel came by for dessert last night. He had a nice piece of peach cobbler while you were off having a nice piece of peaches and cream in the cockpit of that fancy jet," Wanda preaches and finishes with a, "Yeah, I went there!"

Fred's good morning laugh is heard in concert with Wanda's cackle of delight as he twirls, swirls, and dips her low. Again.

The Penn Homestead

The law enforcing men head to former Mayor Jack Cane's place for a bright and early visit.

"What do you know about Jack Cane?"

Damian smirks, "He's a pretty white boy who gets by *because* he's a pretty white boy."

"Cane prettier than me?" Fred smiles.

"Damn, straight Serpico. Jack Cane is a blonde, tanned, golfer-type who's sixty, but looks like he's fifty. He's of the wealthy strata having come by his considerable wealth by marrying above his strata. His wife, Monica Derr Cane is a descendant of Ludwig Derr, founder of Lewisburg. Now add to that bit of lineage the fact that Mr. and Mrs. Cane reside on a sprawling parcel of land once owned by William Penn, the esteemed founder of the Province of Pennsylvania, and you should have a pretty good idea about the esteemed Jack and Monica Cane."

"Don't like them already."

Damian laughs. "Just wait. The family story goes like this. Ludwig Derr purchased tracts of land from William Penn, as did several other settlers. Derr was the only one who befriended local Native Americans when he staked claim, and was the only one whose land was spared attack. One by one the neighboring settlers gave up the fight and put their land up for sale. Derr purchased their tracts at a very reduced price and cobbled them all together to create Derrstown which was later named Lewisburg."

Fred raises a brow at the rambling historian. Damian shrugs his shoulders, "I had to research my hometown for a history assignment at Penn State."

"You aced the assignment?"

"Damn straight, brother. Back to Jack. Prior to his running for mayor, Mr. Cane had no real purpose in life other than satisfying his wife and raising two scholarly offspring. Most people wondered why Abigail Forrester threw her substantial experience and clout behind such an underachiever. Same people are wondering what happened between the two for her to force him out of office. No one buys the BS that Jack resigned due to illness."

"He didn't resign due to illness, although I'm sure he's sick over the shit Abigail has on him," Fred smiles.

"Sweet," Damian smiles.

Fred is blown away by the beauty and expanse of the Cane spread. He is taking in its wonder when the blonde, tanned, golfer-type, Jack Cane approaches. True to form, the man just happens to be carrying a set of golf clubs. Fred mumbles, "You described Jack to a tee – pun intended." The men hold their laughs. Sort of.

Jack extends his hand and offers a genuine smile to Damian, "Good to see you

Captain." He looks at Fred and extends his hand, "Jack Cane."

"Fred Serpico with RFI."

The golfer's genuine smile disappears quickly. He recovers quickly, too, "Damn fine work you people did on The Realm."

Fred nods. Fred wonders about the status of The Realm. Fred tucks away his doubts.

With introductions behind them, Jack addresses the captain, "I assume Abigail Forrester is why you're here, although she was killed in Philadelphia, so it's a bit out of your jurisdiction, Captain."

Fred jumps the hell all over that comment, "I'm just along for the ride, but I suspect Philly PD will be swinging by to ask their own questions about the murder. The captain's here to ask what you know about the file Abigail kept on you."

Jack Cane suddenly looks every minute of his sixty years.

The tense moment is broken by the emergence of Monica Cane from the stately home she shares with her husband. Mrs. Cane is dressed for time on the links and looks displeased that her partner is tied up in conversation. She calls out without any regard to the two men standing with him.

"Jack, you'll need to continue that conversation later, or we'll miss our tee time."

Fred hollers past Jack to his wife, "Sorry for the delay, Mrs. Cane. The captain can have Mr. Cane join him at the police station after his round."

"Police station, whatever for?"

Fred smiles, "The Lewisburg PD wants to ask him about his relationship with Abigail Forrester."

Monica Cane closes the distance between them very quickly, "Are you implying that Jack and Abigail had a relationship other than a professional one?"

Fred offers the pissed-off woman a Serpico smile and a shake of his head.

She starts to lose a bit of her ire.

Fred sends her sky high again, "The suggestion that your husband had a personal relationship does not come from us, Mrs. Cane, it comes from Abigail Forrester—by way of a very detailed account that was found in a file at the murder scene."

"Us?" the captain asks under breath.

"Got carried away," the detective offers.

Monica storms past the men and heads back to the house, "**Jack**, don't say a damn word without a lawyer present. Get in the house."

The man who looks as though he's aged ten years in the last ten minutes follows his wife through the open front door, which she slams damn near off its hinges behind him.

Fred smacks Damian on the shoulder, "Looks as though we teed her off right good. Again, pun intended."

Frizzball funeral.

An RFI detective, a Philly detective, a Lewisburg police captain, a tabloid reporter, a former DC intern, and a paid assassin are going to a funeral. No joke. Some are traveling together—others alone. Some are going for work reasons—others for shits and giggles. The contract killer known as Boston is at the rural cemetery on business. He's parked his Jag on a pathway several over from the final resting place of Ms. Forrester. The Bradley Cooper doppelganger catches a glimpse of himself in the rearview mirror and smirks, "Good looks—the #1 tool of the serial killer's trade. Abigail was all but dead the minute she laid eyes on me…"

Boston had been tailing Abigail Forrester for weeks and knew her daily and nightly routines. He checked his watch then exited his vehicle. He approached the unsuspecting woman as she was coming out of her condo for her daily run to the takeout joint 3.2 miles from her place. "Excuse me, Ms. Forrester…" he intentionally startled her. "I'm sorry, I didn't mean to startle you. My name is Paul Boston. I work for Senator Rodgers."

She raised her hand to shade her eyes from the lowering sun—suddenly very happy she did. *Well, hello, Bradley Cooper.*

"The Senator has asked that I come meet with you about your relocation to Washington. Do you have a few minutes?" Boston's quick smile showed off a swoon-worthy set of dimples.

Abigail's girls budded to attention and she got a bit wet down there just eyeing the devastatingly handsome man standing on her driveway. The answer she wanted to give "Bradley Cooper" was*, I have all the time in the world.* The answer she actually gave him was, "Yes, of course. The thing is I'm just running to get takeout for dinner. I shouldn't be long," she said through her thin-lipped smile.

"I'd be happy to wait in my car, maybe keep you company while you eat," Mr. Exceedingly Handsome offered.

Abigail nodded, a bit too enthusiastically. "Why don't I grab you some takeout, that way I won't have to eat in front of you," she said trying to tamp her excitement.

"I could follow you and we could eat there." Boston tested the waters.

"Actually, I have an appointment with a moving consultant in an hour, so I need to stay close to the condo."

Plan B, he quickly decided. "In that case why don't you grab me tuna on rye." Boston handed her a twenty. "Dinner's on me, or should I say, dinner is on the campaign." Boston dimpled again.

"That's not gonna fly when I'm in charge," she laughed. "I'll be back in fifteen."

Boston headed back to wait in his Jag. "Too bad I can't handle you now, but thanks for the info about your appointment with the moving consultant."

The contract killer enjoyed dinner with his soon-to-be-victim. "You're from Scranton," he small talked.

Abigail groaned, "Don't remind me."

He laughed. "Philly is a better fit for you?"

"It was. I'm looking forward to being in DC again. I've been gone a long time." She paused. She pushed, "Maybe you'll take me around town, make sure I'm seen at the right places."

He smiled, "Whatever you need to get settled back in. Have you found a place to live?"

"Not yet. I might have to stay in a hotel for a while."

"I'll give you a call tomorrow with a list of realtors who are very plugged in," he offered.

Abigail beamed, "Perfect."

There wouldn't be a tomorrow for
Abigail Forrester…

He straddled her chest locking her arms beneath his knees and silencing her with a hand to her mouth. He put a loaded gun to her head, "If you make a sound, I will kill you. Do you understand?"

She nodded.

"I came to deliver a message. You need to listen to everything I have to say. I am going to gag you and tape your mouth shut. I will not hurt you if you cooperate. Do you understand?"

She nodded—opened her mouth—moaned pitifully.

He put a pair of silk panties in—taped her mouth shut—exhaled fully.

"Open your eyes, Abigail. Very good. Turner Rodgers does not want you in DC. He is taking back his block. Do you understand?"

She nodded.

"The Realm wants you dead."

The killer pulls himself from memory lane and gets back to the task at hand. He scans his surroundings before looking through a set of binoculars. He easily identifies people who fall into the category of family members and friends, "Not many, no surprise," and one or two female politicians, "The labia set was of no use to you, were they Abigail?" He laughs. He scans. He finds a group of five standing separate from the assembled flock. He eyes them through his lens. "Fred Serpico of RFI and ……. Captain Damian Johnson of Lewisburg PD ……. hailed heroes from the Cappa Escobar and Micky Strong days—and let's not forget Serpico's notoriety from the supposed takedown of The

Realm. Premature accolades for you Detective Serpico, although you did do your fair share of damage to the organization."

Boston takes his telephoto lens and begins snapping pictures of the others with them. He uploads several shots into a facial recognition program and gets immediate hits on two of the three, "Detective Theodore Brothers out of the Philly PD, and Penny Meehan a tabloid reporter with *Kiss and Tell* out of Lewisburg." The last of the group of five takes a few minutes to process, but he gets a hit, "Kathleen 'Katie' O'Brien, a 1999 intern for Congressman Turner Rodgers."

Boston kicks back and waits through the service and while the mourners disperse. He keeps his eyes trained on the laggers, "Interesting group." He watches as the reporter introduces the intern to the others. "Makes sense. Katie O'Brien is the odd duck out—the rest all swim together. Wonder how Meehan and O'Brien know each other?" Boston slides his camera into its case, puts it onto the floor behind the passenger seat, and leaves the cemetery.

Boston is nearly back in DC when he places a call, "I thought you said RFI was pulled from the case ...... yeah, well, Fred Serpico was at the funeral. He had cohorts with him, Captain Damian Johnson from the Lewisburg PD, Detective Ted Brothers from the Philly PD, Penny Meehan, the gossip reporter from *Kiss and Tell*, and Kathleen 'Katie' O'Brien, a 1999 intern from Turner's office, from when Abigail Forrester was there."

He listens for a minute, then disconnects from 'his handler'. He begins planning his next assignment. "Maybe I should rent a place in Pennsylvania. Sure would cut down on the wear and tear on the Jag," he laughs.

Biden's on Main
The Scranton-located namesake establishment of former Vice President, Joe Biden, is packed elbow to elbow with the lunch crowd. The walls of the exposed brick face, glass, and brass joint are covered with framed pictures, newspaper articles, and magazine covers of the hometown politician. If something has a connection to the former Scrantonian, it's on proud display at Biden's on Main.

The men and women grab a table in the back and order beers all around. They raise their pints in celebration of those who survived the wrath of Abigail Forrester, then place their order for the 'award-winning' Biden's fish 'n chips.

Fred is seated next to Katie O'Brien who leans in and says, "I really wish I had time to do a jig on the bitch's grave."

Fred raises his beer, "Geez Katie, tell me how you really feel."

She tosses him a wicked grin, "Geez Fred, I just did." The two of them bust a gut laughing.

Penny is seated on the other side of Fred. She nudges him, “See, I told you it would be a jig.”

Fred raises his beer, “Never doubted you, Penny.”

She tosses him a knowing grin, “It’s that investigative gene the two of us share.” They summarily clink their glasses.

Ted Brothers is seated on the other side of Penny. She nudges him, “Feel like sharing any information on the bitch’s murder?”

Ted raises his beer, “Nice try, but I don’t Kiss and Tell.”

She tosses him a dazzling grin, “Well, you’re hot, so if you’d like to do the kissing part, I’ll never tell.”

The two of them clink glasses.

Damian, who’s been listening to the ‘Round Robin’ of verbal shenanigans, pops a French fry into his mouth before anyone nudges him into the fun.

Under oath.

Gretchen returns all rosy pink from her daily three-mile trek around and through Hufnagle Park. This morning she enjoyed the company of Leavy as she 'walked her ass off'. The women head to the kitchen for tall glasses of iced orange juice, then take seats on the leather couch.

Leavy points to Gretchen's very big, perfectly round baby bump, "I'm kind of surprised at how fast you walk. By the way, are you gestating a basketball in honor of 77, or what?"

Mama-to-be gently pats her bump, "I know, right? Aside from the round baby mound and happy-time boobs, nothing has changed physically during this pregnancy, and though I don't run anymore, nothing's changed in the walking department, either. I credit my long legs."

"Yeah, well, I was hauling ass and panting to keep up with you."

Gretchen raises her glass, "I do believe those were the words you used last night in the guest suite with Manuel, hauling ass and panting to keep up."

Leavy spits her juice at Gretchen whose baby mound responds with a flourish of elbows and knees. The women crack-up, then do it all over again when Gretchen pees a bit in her pants and scurries from the room, calling over her shoulder, “Don’t make me laugh!” She returns in a new pair of leggings and warm rag socks. “Please keep in mind that pregnant women and bladders are enemies during the last trimester.”

Leavy goes silent for a minute, then wades into a conversation, “Gretchen, I want to ask you something, but if I overstep, tell me, okay?”

“Sure.”

“I’ve been wondering about you and Malcolm because it seems like it all happened so fast between the two of you.”

Gretchen nods.

“If you don’t mind telling me, when did you fall in love with Malcolm?”

Gretchen smiles wide, “Honestly, I think it was the very first time I laid eyes on him. There was this thing about him, and it unleashed this sex-vixen in me. I flirted shamelessly with that amazingly gorgeous man behind the locked doors of a prison. Can you imagine?”

Leavy nods, “Well, yeah, I mean look at him.”

Gretchen giggles, “I know, right?”

Leavy isn’t finished with her questions, “And when did you know you were going to have sex with him?”

Gretchen's smile widens, "The first time he said my name." She gives her head a gentle shake and runs her fingers through her cropped hair at the memory of it. "I came here to ask him for a favor. He leaned low and said, 'I hope that's code for you wanting me to bang your brains out, Gretchen'. I tell you, that was it for me. I swooned. No really, I felt my very first swoon at the sound of my name rolling off his lips."

Leavy totally gets it. "And when did you know you'd marry him?"

Gretchen puts her hand to her heart and pulls a deep breath, "The first time he gentled me in bed."

Leavy waves her hand to move some air across her face, "Holy shit, Gretchen, it's getting hot in here, maybe we should change subjects."

The missus giggles a bit then takes Leavy's hand in hers, "Are you in an okay space to tell me a few things about Manuel and John?"

She nods, "Actually, I think if you asked a few questions it might help me process everything."

Gretchen turns her body toward Leavy, "I'm gonna lawyer you, that way you'll drill down to the facts and not get hung up on all the self-analysis we women tend to torture ourselves with."

Leavy readjusts herself on the couch and prepares for her direct examination by Attorney Gretchen Mitchell.

"Did Manuel save you from a kidnapping?"

"He rescued me after I had been kidnapped and was about to be shipped out of the country."

"Where were you when you were kidnapped?"

"I was working with John, Fred, and Steve at an off-site FICA workplace called Netti Barn. At the time, FBI Special Agent John Maxwell was my boss. He was training me to take over the cyber huntress job vacated by Joy Ann Watts—you know her as Joy Fiancetti. John, Fred, and Steve were providing backup assistance to Rocco Fiancetti who had taken into protective custody the #1 and #2 ranked cyber huntresses, Joy Ann Watts and Annie Maxwell-Mahoney. Annie is John's daughter and Fred's sort-of-stepdaughter, so it was a very intense time for both men. Annie was in hiding and was being hunted hard by The Realm." Leavy stops to laugh, "Geez, Gretchen, you know who all these people are. I'm acting like I'm a witness in a courtroom."

Gretchen doesn't break role, "Continue, Agent Leavy."

"No one, except Fred Serpico, expected The Realm to make a move on the #3 ranked cyber huntress. Unfortunately, he figured it out as I was being dragged into the kidnapper's car."

Gretchen places her hand on Leavy's leg, "Do you need to stop?"

Leavy shakes her head, "No, please, let's do this. I've never dealt with any of it."

Gretchen notices movement from over Leavy's shoulder. Manuel locks eyes with her and shakes his head.

The lawyer continues the questioning. "Okay, so you've been kidnapped, then what?"

"I was taken to an abandoned warehouse and kept for a couple of days. The morning I was scheduled to be shipped out of the country on an LNG tanker headed to Antonio Alvarez in Peru…"

Breath wooshes from Gretchen, "A vile human being. You know he hired someone to kill me?"

A penny-dropped memory hits Leavy. "Oh, Gretchen, we shouldn't be talking about this, you're pregnant."

The mom-to-be waves Leavy's concern away, "That killer is old news; there's been another since then. Continue, please."

Leavy laughs at Gretchen's nonchalance. "A team of FBI agents who'd been undercover inside the Alvarez organization kidnapped me away from The Realm. Within hours Manuel and I were back at John's farmhouse, and for the next two months we stayed hidden in a secret room behind a set of paneled walls. John knew he had to get me out of the country, so he quit his job at FICA and arranged for us to go into hiding with Rocco and Joy at The Compound.

Manuel joined us there within a week's time. While we were holed up behind that paneled wall, Manuel was listed as AWOL from FICA and had an $8 Million bounty on his head, and..." Leavy turns wetting eyes away from Gretchen.

"You fell in love with Manuel—from the very beginning." It could have been a question, but it wasn't.

Leavy drops her head and welcomes the silent tears that fall. "Yes, and it intensified while we were living at The Compound."

Gretchen takes Leavy's hand, "Why did you stay with John? I'm not judging, Leavy, just wondering is all."

"John wanted me. Manuel wanted Dominique, and then he wanted Muriel. It was very unfair of me to stay with John knowing how I felt about Manuel, but the thing is, John never put any pressure on us to be anything more than what we were—two people who had a 'thing'. John Maxwell is a good man, but he is a fractured man. He's lived his entire adult life undercover and was never allowed to share the deepest, truest parts of himself with anyone. If John had feelings for me, real feelings, he never said so. And as for me, I couldn't love John because I was in love with Manuel—I have been since the day we met." The emotions she's been barely keeping in check are released.

Manuel has had enough. He knew it was important for her to get out the feelings she'd kept buried, but… He goes to Leavy and gently pulls her from the couch and wraps her tight against him, "This is where you belong, Leavy. It's where you always should have been." He kisses her cheek and whispers, "I returned to Dominique because she was pregnant with my baby, but I wanted you every minute of every day since I met you. It was torture seeing you with John. I hate to say this about myself, but I used Muriel as a distraction from you. It didn't work. It never could have worked."

Gretchen hoists herself from the couch, places a hand onto Manuel's shoulder and leaves the couple alone.

From Professor to Poindexter.

Ted Brothers gives Fred a set of house keys as they leave Biden's, "Have Damian drop you off. If you need to go anywhere, Janelle's Jeep is in the garage, fridge is stocked, and I left you a box of files in my office. Heads up, I work cases a little different, Fred, so check the stuff on my desk first."

Damian and Fred park in front of a modified log cabin home on a quiet street with similarly built homes. "Didn't expect this," Fred says as he shuts the car door.

The rambling historian can't help himself, "Actually, Drexel Hill, Pennsylvania, is known as New Sweden because of the distinctly identifiable log cabin architecture of colonial Swedes. Over by Darby Creek there's a log house that's supposedly the oldest of its kind in North America." Damian takes a surveying look at Ted's place, "This house has an original log structure tucked within the additions. I bet the inside part of the logging is going to be something else."

Fred taps Damian on the shoulder, "I'm sure gonna miss these history lessons, Captain. Come on, let's take a peek inside."

Both men emit a whistle when they get there. The place is **all man**. The original log structure houses a family room that has what can only be described as man-furniture. Distressed wood and worn black leather recliners and couch face an impressive river-rock fireplace above which hangs a 60" flat screen TV. Big block end tables and a matching coffee table chunk away big block swaths of the room. There isn't a damned doily, or bowl of potpourri, or drink coaster in sight.

"A man lives here," the two men grunt.

Next to the most worn of the two chairs is a wrought iron floor lamp and a rack full of magazines. Fred lifts a couple, "Mathematics Digest?" A dawning takes hold. "Oh, Jesus, I'm leaving the world of history for the world of math," Fred shakes his head. "How did I not know The Keystone State is the boring-ass academic state?"

Damian is quick to respond, "Math sucks, man, history on the other hand, that's some interesting shit."

Fred slaps Damian on the shoulder as he walks past, "Sorry man, did you say something because I think I fell asleep."

"Ass-wipe," Damian says as he follows Fred to Ted's office just off the log room.

Ted Brothers' fascination with math becomes immediately evident after a quick walkthrough.

"Detective Brothers has a PhD in Applied Mathematics and Computational Science from Northeastern," Fred announces. "Wonder why the divergence from math to murder?" Fred reads the framed and hung degrees and citations of note as he heads to Ted's desk. "Hey, Damian, look at these."

Captain Johnson reviews the documents. "Venn diagrams and probability studies. Interesting, damn interesting. Not just the use of Venn diagrams, but how they are actually isolating comparatives." Damian studies them a few more minutes, "These are cool, I never would have thought to use a Venn."

Fred takes back the diagrams, "The head of our cyber division uses Venns, so I have some working knowledge of it, but…" He studies them a bit more, "Wait until we get the Dominique and Celia interview information from Granger; Ted will be in mathematical heaven when he gets to load that shit into the closed curves and see which comparisons hit the center one."

"Okay, Fred, I'm heading back to Lewisburg. I'll let you know if and when I schedule a chit-chat with the former mayor, although I'm sure his wife will keep him busy with her own questions for the foreseeable future. As for wives, thanks for winding mine up this morning. I'm glad you aren't going to be around tonight."

Fred slaps Damian on the shoulder, "Glad I could help. Try not to bore Wanda to death with your history lectures, Professor."

"Wanda is a physician's assistant, remember? We tend to play doctor," the officer's smile widens.

"I know. Your walls are on the thin side," the investigator's smile widens.

Fred spends a couple of hours reviewing Ted's files and settles on a list of questions that is nearly identical to the mathematician's. There's one word at the bottom of Ted's list that is also on Fred's list, **woods**. Both detectives are wondering whether Celia Brettenvue's murderer came through the woods that surround Granger Mitchell's estate. Fred places two calls while still at Ted's desk. The first is to Granger Mitchell. "This is Fred Serpico."

"What can I do for you, Detective?"

"I'd like to spend some time at the Carriage House…work a few things through."

"Stop by the Cottage when you arrive."

The second call is to RFI ground specialist, Mike Monopoli, "I could use your help in Philly. Be here tomorrow and be ready to trek."

Old Estate Road

Fred and Ted wait as Granger Mitchell unlocks the Carriage House and deactivates an alarm system. He gives Fred a set of keys and the security codes, then leaves. The detectives begin an immediate back and forth.

"How did the killer get into the Carriage House..."

"The Feds were supposedly sitting in their vehicle with visuals on both entry points..."

"But the killer got into a building that requires key and security code access..."

"Did the victim or the detail leave the doors unlocked..."

"Did the FBI security detail help the killer get in?"

Fred makes a call to Manuel, "I've got you on speaker so Ted Brothers can hear. I need you to step back into your FBI days for a minute. Let me recap the situation for a second, then I'll get to my questions. There was a 4-hour check-in schedule on Celia Brettenvue. The detail did an 8 PM check, said it was lights out right after that, so they decided to skip the midnight and 4 AM checks. They found the victim dead at 8 AM. Here are my questions: Is it SOP for the **agent** to physically lock the door and set the alarm on their way out, or is it left up to the **subject** to flip the lock and set security? Is there ever a time when locks and alarms aren't set, for instance if the detail is sitting right outside and has visuals on the points of entry?"

"SOP is for the Feds to do the physical securing of a location. Further, there is no justification for the agents to leave the site accessible, especially if they'd planned to skip two check-ins. Everything about this is off – that's why Remington removed them from the scene and Webber discharged them from service. I'm gonna do some follow-up on this, Fred."

"Thanks. Before you go, let the team know there's a meeting scheduled at 275 for 7 PM tomorrow. They should be ready to participate and stay for several hours."

"Will do."

Ted waits a fraction of a second then brings it, "This bullshit falls way outside the probability range of a coincidental set of circumstances. The night Celia Brettenvue was murdered, her security detail **didn't** do SOP time checks, **may not have** locked the doors or set alarms, **didn't** see the killer come from the street or through the trees, **on the exact** night that there were multiple breaches in protocol allowing easy entry and egress at a Federally protected facility."

Fred smiles wide, "You know, I think I'm gonna like working with a mathematical genius. Come on Poindexter, let's look at the Celia Brettenvue files Granger and McKay left for us."

Locked and loaded.

Boston starts his day watching the Drexel Hill home of Ted Brothers. "Let's see if the RFI detective is still lodging with the Philly detective." Within several minutes he makes the confirmation, "Fred Serpico wasn't in town for the funeral of Abigail Forrester. He's still working the case he was discharged from. That means one of two things: RFI is pulling a fast one on Stacy Remington; or **she** is pulling a fast one on her boss. I need some intel from inside the Bureau." He places a call only to disconnect it immediately, "I'll call back. My subjects are on the move."

Serpico and Brothers leave the log cabin and head in two different directions. Boston figures the Philly detective is heading to PPD so he follows Serpico—directly to the gated community at Old Estate Road. He drives past, "Been there, done that," he laughs. "Next stop, Lewisburg." He gets onto I-476N, cranks Springteen's *Streets of Philadelphia,* and plans the next part of his day.

Lewisburg

The paid assassin arrives at Hufnagle Park just as Mrs. Mayor and another woman finish their walkthrough. He snaps a few pictures of the mystery woman, uploads them into a facial recognition program, and confirms that the beautiful babe is former FICA Agent, Hannah Leavy. "That's the second RFI team member who's supposedly **not** on this case," Boston scoffs.

He spends a few minutes riding a very cold park bench and is rewarded handsomely for his efforts, "Bingo!" He trains his eyes on the black Land Rover that exists from beneath the building at 275 Market Street. He immediately recognizes the passenger as the hipster dude who pulled the fire alarm at Mitchell and Morgan the night Boston and his associate were there to steal the Celia and Dominique Brettenvue files. Boston practically snarls his recognition of the driver of the Land Rover, "The third RFI team member supposedly **not** working the case, former FICA Agent, Manuel Xavier. Too bad I didn't find you when there was an $8 million bounty on your head."

After another few minutes in the cold, Boston packs up and heads to *Kiss and Tell*. The intel he's gathered since getting his assignment showed three very interesting things about the trash reporter: Penny Meehan spent recent time in DC snooping into the lives of Abigail Forrester and Senator Turner Rodgers, she is **very** *good* at what she does, and she poses a **very** real danger to the GOP candidate. "You aren't the biggest threat to our getting

Rodgers elected as President, but you've made yourself known to the people who call the shots. That was a mistake, Ms. Meehan, a deadly mistake."

Boston waits until Penny breaks for lunch then follows her into Chip's across the street from the *Kiss and Tell* offices. He gives the pretty military-buff woman a l.o.n.g. look. He pegs the woman at 5'8" and 135 pounds of lean muscle. Her dark hair is near military-cut, and her curious dark brown eyes are darting around Chip's, searching for anomalies. Boston knows he's an anomaly, and she is going to find him—correction: she's already found him. He makes a preemptive move toward the woman sitting at the counter, "Excuse me, I noticed you looking at me while I was looking at you. I think we may have met, you're ex-military, right?"

Penny swivels her counter stool and offers her hand in greeting, "Sergeant Penelope Meehan, Army Reserves, and you?"

"Paul Boston, ma'am, Marine through and through."

"Take a seat Paul. If you're the type to take food suggestions, you might want to try the chicken parmesan salad on garlic toast. It's to die for," Penny shoots a smile that doesn't quite meet her eyes then goes back to her lunch. Boston waits until the non-communicative reservist-reporter finishes her food, offers her nod of goodbye, and gets back inside the *Kiss and Tell* office. He finishes his sandwich, pays his tab, and leaves. The man on a reconnaissance mission drives to the condo complex where Penny Meehan lives. "Hadwen–A Residential Community," he reads the welcome sign, then takes the turn-in and begins his assessment. "Nice. Quiet. Four side-by-side unit structures on either side of the street and well-spaced from one another. Landscaping between the units offers some cover." He drives by Penny's place, "Last structure. Last condo. Nice tree line on the far side and along the back."

He drives to the end of the street and hangs a right, then another right. "No houses directly in the back of her space. A good amount of tree cover between the street and her backyard." He goes the length of the street then spins around, "A couple single-family houses, well-spaced from one another." He pulls off to the side of the road and sits for several minutes, "Quiet street. Not many cars. No one out and about." He notices two cut-through paths heading into the treed area, "Most likely for walking." He gets out of his car and goes walking. "If I follow the path in and around, I'll end up back on the street where I've parked."

He doesn't follow the path. He pushes through the thick of things and ends at the boundary of Penny's backyard. He finds a place to sit, "Nice, easy access. The house is about

200' from where the backyard abuts the wooded area. The whole damned back of the place is windows and sliders. Easy in and out." He runs images of his victim through his head, "No. No. Penny Meehan **is not** a victim—she's an adversary. This one is former military. She'll put up a damned good fight. Better not get up close and personal with this one." He sits. He scans. He makes his plan. "I'm coming locked and loaded for you, Penny Meehan."

Philly

Ted Brothers has been thinking about the sassy woman who offered to kiss him the other day at Biden's. "It's been awhile since I've thought about a woman," he admits to the space around him. He reflexively touches his wedding band with his thumb, and he's reminded for the millionth time how quickly life can go to shit. His mind floods with thoughts of Janelle, with the loss of his wife, his partner, his friend. "It's been awhile since I've been with a woman," he says to no one—maybe to someone. He makes hard work on the ring he still wears, touching and spinning, touching and spinning. Makes hard work of pushing away the pain that wants to take hold and make a mess of things again.

His mind fills with thoughts of Penny, "I can't get you out of my head. I don't want to." Ted knows he's going to kiss the lips that Penny offered— he's pretty sure she knows it too after he places the call.

"It's Ted." He thinks he feels Penny's smile through the phone when he says, "I'll be in Lewisburg tonight on business, I thought I'd stop by your place when I'm done."

"I think I'll be there when you do, Ted."

Well, statistically speaking.

The penthouse is packed to the rafters. Malcolm and Gretchen, Manuel and Leavy, Randy and Peyton, Damian Johnson and Ted Brothers are all in attendance. They are awaiting the arrival of Fred, who went to get Mike from the airport.

The living room furniture has been moved toward the window and positioned in a U-meeting style. The room is in the grips of laughter when the RFI men step from the privacy elevator. "Probably something The Kid said," Fred tells Mike as they approach. Greetings and introductions are made, then it's down to business.

Manuel kicks off the meeting, "We are going to get to our recaps in a minute." He hands out two sheets of paper to each attendee. "The first page is a summary prepared by Stacy Remington. She gave that to me when she relieved RFI from the Forrester and Brettenvue cases, and sent a second copy to me, here. It's the basis for the Tango and Octopus research Randy and Peyton did last week. If there's anything to add to the summary, or any talking points about it, let's hold it to the end."

There are nodding heads all around.

"I'd like to spend some time on the second sheet. It came this morning by regular mail with no return address. It was sent by Stacy, despite her being under an RFI communication ban issued from FBI brass. You will note that this sheet looks like a series of questions. They are, but they are also assignments. Director Remington is working these questions, and she wants us working them, too. Some of the questions have been on our radar, so let's review them.

"One: Why was Director Remington forced to remove RFI from the Forrester and Brettenvue cases? Two: Who has a vested interest in keeping this case from being solved? Three: Turner Rodgers? We could spend hours on this one. Four: Octopus? Five: Who is The Body? Six: If the leaders of The Realm are under arrest then who is running this organization? Seven: Have the leaders been replaced? Eight: Did we arrest the leaders?"

"Fuck," Fred whispers, as he makes his way to the bank of windows.

Everyone else remains silent.

After a few minutes, The Justice raises her hand. Manuel laughs as he calls on her, "Do college students still raise their hands?"

Peyton shrugs, "I do. I'm sorry for the interruption, but I noticed something on the Director's Octopus summary that I find interesting. May I share?"

Manuel sits. Peyton stands. “While The Kid and I were wowing you with the Tango, I told you that the original dance had influences from the German Waltz, Czech Polka, Polish Mazurka, Bohemian Schottische, Cuban Habanera, African Candombe and the Argentinian Milonga.”

“G, C, P, B, C, A, A,” Ted says.

Peyton squeals, “Yes! You get it!”

Fred interrupts his window-processing with an over the shoulder comment, “Whatever Ted just got, it’s probably because he has a PhD in Applied Mathematics and Computational Science. He analyzes everything in a Poindexter kind of way,”

“Cool. So it jumps out at you, too?”

Ted smiles, “It’s obvious.”

Manuel stares the two of them down, “Would one of you care to share what the hell you’re talking about?”

“German, Czech, Polish, Bohemian, Cuban, African, and Argentinian,” Peyton says.

“G, C, P, B, C, A, A,” Ted says.

“Guatemala, Columbia, Peru, Brazil, Chile, Africa, and Argentina,” Peyton and Ted say in unison. Ted finishes it up for the others, “Seven of the eight Realm leaders, or supposed leaders, come from countries that begin with the letter of the countries that developed the Tango. Suggesting coincidence is a factor in these countries, these initials, and these individuals being involved in The Realm and Tango falls far outside the parameters of reasonability."

"Far, far outside," Peyton chimes in.

Ted continues, "In the overall scheme of things this information may not be worth much to our murder investigations, but it presents solid evidence that the name of the dance is integral to the impetus of The Realm."

There is stunned silence—Randy breaks it, "My babe is smokin' smart, and now she's got a shadow of smartness."

Captain Johnson is still shaking his head at Randy when he takes over the floor for a recap of the interviews he and Fred did. "Our overall assessments aren't based on intellect..."

"Objection!" Fred shouts.

Damian laughs and continues, "But they are as follows: Topher Griffin is a broken man. He expressed his regret that he wasn't the one who killed Abigail. The only alibi he offered is that she wasn't torched to death, which would have been his preferred method of homicide; Penny Meehan freely admits she hated Abigail enough to kill her, but at the time of the murder, the reporter was working on a hatchet piece that would have killed Abigail in the press; Jack Cane, affectionately referred to as 'Mr. Kinky Pants' by the murder victim, may have had reason to kill Abigail **if** he knew about the salacious file she had on him. I will be following up with him **if** he survives the wrath of Mrs. Jack

Cane, who may also have had a similar motive for getting rid of Abigail Forrester."

Manuel concludes his part of the meeting with the following. "Assignments will be handed out, but these are the basics. There will be deep dives on the 8 supposed leaders of The Realm. We need to figure out who The Body is, and what Tango is. We will also be diving into Benton Brettenvue, Celia Brettenvue, Dominique Brettenvue, Abigail Forrester, and every named block on her Tower of Power. Whatever assignment you get—whatever information you find—see if it circles back to Turner Rodgers. It sure would be good to know if the presidential candidate is part of The Realm."

Ted approaches Fred at the window. "Sorry for the interruption."

"What's up Ted?"

"Tell Mike he can camp out on the sofa in the upstairs den. And there's a chance that I won't be home tonight..."

Fred slaps the man's shoulder, "Then I expect to see you appropriately unwound tomorrow, Detective."

"Well, statistically speaking …"

"Good god, man, leave statistics out of this one," Fred says through a groan.

Before

The intended victim of a homicide arrives home a little after 9 PM. Boston is parked on a street behind the condo complex watching her movements through a set of night vision binoculars. He waits until the upstairs fills with light before heading through the tree line behind her corner unit. The sniper takes position at the fire sight he set earlier in the day and settles in. He checks his rifle, checks his sights, checks the landmarks, checks the neighbors' units, puts his rifle next to him, then hunkers down. It's close to 11 PM when, one by one, the condo units go dark—except for hers. "Perfect."

The assassin shifts in his spot when she returns to the first floor. He follows her movements through the living room, into kitchen area, down a hallway. She turns on overhead lights as she moves along. "Perfect." He assesses, "She's towel drying her hair, she must have showered. It looks like she's in for the night—black leggings and a sleeveless tee." A gust of bitter air pushes hard against him. He notices a slight shake in his hand, "Fucking cold." He wills her to find a place to sit, but she moves about, tidying this and straightening that. A handful of minutes pass before she perches on the sofa and picks up a book.

Several more minutes pass, "Looks like she's staying put." Boston raises his gun. "Plenty of space between the top of the sofa back and her left scapula. She'll be dead before she hits the ground." He takes a breath, releases it, then squeezes the trigger —— just as a car pulls to a stop at her unit. Boston hightails it back through the trees, hops into his car, and speeds away, not knowing the status of his victim.

After

A bullet blows through Penny's condo window just as Ted Brothers arrives. He bolts from his car and runs to the front door, already on the phone with Lewisburg PD dispatch, "Detective Brothers, PPD, I need an ambulance at 111 Hadwen Parkway," then he sees her, "for a GSW. Contact Captain Johnson." He simultaneously disconnects and shouts, "Penny!" The detective kicks in her front door and is at her side within a minute of the shot. Her torso is already covered in blood. He pulls her to the floor, checks for a pulse, and for breathing. He begins CPR.

Captain Johnson answers a call from Lewisburg dispatch. He listens then yells to Fred, "Penny Meehan's been shot! Ted called it in." The men are in the elevator going down before Damian finishes his sentence.

Ted is climbing into the ambulance just as Fred and Damian arrive. He yells to them before the door closes, "The shot came from the back of the condo. Check the tree line."

Fred is just about to call Mike when he and Manuel arrive on scene. The RFI men check inside and outside of Penny's unit, while Captain

Johnson heads to Mrs. Margaret Shanahan who is standing at her front door holding tight to her Popcorn furball. She smiles sweetly as the captain approaches. “I’m grateful you came to help our sweet Penny.” The captain offers the woman a place in his arms, holds her for a minute then instructs, “You should go back inside, ma’am. I’ll stop over before I leave.”

Fred and Manuel find Ted Brothers standing vigil outside the operating room. The new friend places his hand onto Ted’s shoulder, “Any news on Penny?”

“She coded in the ER. A medical team pushed her gurney past with a damned doctor straddling her chest and performing CPR. It’s fucking bad, Fred.”

“What can we do?”

“Tell me she’s gonna make it.”

Penny makes it through surgery and through the rest of the night. Ted is allowed inside the ICU for a minute or two, every hour or so. He is just coming out when Mike arrives with an overnight bag, “Thought you might want to change.” He hands off another bag to Fred, “Coffees and sandwiches.” The men eat while Mike talks, “Do either of you know if Penny has family? We can’t find anything that indicates she does.”

Ted lifts his shoulders.

Fred answers, "No family."

Mike nods. "Okay. Let me update you on what happened last night after you left the shooting scene. The assassin was in wait for some time—maybe a few hours, and it looks as though he made a couple of trips in and out of his fire sight. I canvassed a segment of the neighborhood and talked to a guy who said his wife mentioned a strange vehicle being parked on a side street earlier in the day. The wife went out of town on business, so we'll talk to her as soon as we can. If the guy parked on the street is the shooter, then he returned last night, got set in his spot, and waited for the condo units to go quiet. We checked with the elderly next-door neighbor. She said she turned her lights out at 11 PM, and within minutes she heard Penny's door being kicked in. Ted, your call to dispatch came in at 11:11."

Mike takes a sip of his coffee then asks, "What happened when you pulled up?"

"I got out of my car just after a bullet came tearing through the front window of the condo. I contacted LPD and made my way to the unit. As I approached I could see Penny half on, half off the couch. I kicked in the door, pulled her to the floor, checked her vitals, and began CPR. She was out of it and never came back into it," Ted bows his head, "Fucking assholes shooting women. I can't fucking escape it." Ted tempers himself when a nurse speaks his name, "Excuse me, are you Ted Brothers?"

The men brace themselves for bad news, "Yes, ma'am, I'm Detective Ted Brothers."

The nurse touches his arm, "Penny woke briefly and finger-spelled your name in sign language. I thought you might be Ted; I've seen you in and out of the unit. Penny's not my patient, but I know how to sign, so her nurse got me. She's fighting, Ted. She was in really bad shape when she got here, but she made it through surgery, and she's pushing toward the corner. What we need now is for her to turn the corner." The nurse touches his arm before leaving.

Ted smiles wide, "If she wakes again, will you tell her I'm here and I'm not going anywhere?"

The nurse shares Ted's smile, signs something with her fingers, then goes back inside the unit.

Philly

While Ted Brothers stays at Penny's side, Fred Serpico heads to the log cabin in Drexel Hill. "Okay. Four women. Dead or almost dead. All of them are connected by The Realm. Take it step by step. First homicide. Abigail Forrester." He starts reworking her case. He reads Ted's reports then reviews crime scene photos. He reads forensic reports then reviews crime scene photos. He reads his notes then reviews crime scene photos. "Something about the crime scene photos is bugging the shit out of me. What is it? Where is it?" He abandons all else and focuses solely on the photos. On a flip-through, one of them grabs his attention. "The legal pad on the kitchen table." Fred ignores the names on the pad and eyes the business card sitting on top. "Premium Movers. The card was on **top** of the pad. When did Abigail get that card?"

Fred calls Premium Movers and asks to speak with Brenna Campbell. A very chipper young voice comes onto the line, "Hi, this is Brenna, how may I help you?"

"Ms. Campbell, my name is Detective Fred Serpico. I'm working on the Abigail Forrester murder..."

"And you want to talk with me because I was with Ms. Forrester the day she was killed?"

"You're sure you were with her **that** day?"

"Certain," Brenna says in a most certain way.

"Are you available to meet with me today?"

"I'm in the office, stop by anytime."

Philadelphia

Brenna Campbell is a thirty-year-old hippy chic woman who subtly owns her space. She is quite lovely; most would say she is a natural beauty. Her dark brown hair hits just below her shoulders; her hazel eyes are heavily flecked with gold; and her smile reveals a set of near perfect teeth, the front two of which have a tiny overlap she often brushes with the tip of her tongue.

Fred extends his hand, “Thank you for meeting me, Ms. Campbell.”

“It’s Brenna. And it’s no problem. I thought someone would have been by sooner.”

“Because you were there the day she died?”

“No. Because **he** was there the day she died.”

“He was there? Who is he, Brenna?”

“The Bradley Cooper lookalike. When I arrived for my appointment, Ms. Forrester was wrapping up a meeting—with a very hot, very handsome man. When she escorted the man out, they exchanged a few flirty words.”

“And you heard those words?”

She nods, the jingle, jangle of several earrings give musical introduction to her big tell. “He said something like, ‘It was a pleasure meeting you, Abigail, I’ll be seeing you again.’ Ms. Forrester sort of panted the word ‘—soon.’ He smiled and winked then said, ‘Sooner than you think.’”

“Any chance you heard the ‘hot and handsome’ man’s name?”

Brenna smiles wide, “I’m not sure, exactly, but when he was walking away, he answered his cell phone with one word: Boston.”

Old Estate Road

Fred leaves Premium Movers and goes directly to the Carriage House to meet up with Mike. He drives the RFI grounds specialist out of the gated community to a street that runs parallel to Old Estate Road. Mike assesses as Fred drives. "The abutting streets are separated by at least three-quarters of a mile of woods in all directions. That doesn't make for an easy trek, especially at night. If this is the route our killer used to get to the Carriage House, you can narrow your search to someone with trekking chops, maybe ex-military, or someone with survivalist training."

Mike hops out of the Jeep. Fred heads back to Old Estate Road to wait. It's a little more than an hour before Mike emerges from the woods. He meets Fred inside the Carriage House and hands off his cell phone. "I took a series of pictures on my way through." Mike narrates as Fred checks the shots on Mike's cell. "The killer took some time in the woods marking a trail. He **did not** do that work on the night he killed Celia Brettenvue."

"Reflective tape?" Fred asks.

"Yeah. Small, folded strips of yellow tape are fastened to east-facing branches on inward approach spaced about 50' apart. The tree marking begins where you dropped me off and ends a few hundred feet from the property line.

The strips were put at a level that suggests our killer is 6'2" give or take. The killer has been in those woods on multiple occasions and probably knows the route by memory now. Whoever he is, he's trained in ground traverse. Add to that the up close and personal strangulation of two women, I think we are dealing with ex-military."

Fred flips through the pictures, again. "Why didn't he take the tape? It's evidence. Leaving it not only proves how he got to the Carriage House, but it might also provide forensics."

Mike leans back against a counter and pulls a swig of water. "Maybe he plans on coming back."

"Well, fuck."

Welcome back.

Two days pass before Penny wakes. When she does, she finds Ted asleep in a chair that's been pulled close to her bed. His hand is resting on her arm—that she moves—ever so slightly. His eyes shoot open, and he bolts upright. A w.i.d.e. smile cuts his face, as he leans close. He places his hand on top of her head and runs his thumb back and forth across her brow, "Welcome back."

Penny sends him a weak smile. "Shot?" she whispers.

Ted nods.

"Bad?" she croaks.

Ted nods, "But you're working through it. I'm so glad to see those beautiful eyes of yours, Penny." He leans down and places a kiss onto her temple. "I'm gonna go get a nurse to check you out. I'll be right back."

"Promise?"

"Promise," he smiles. He's gone for a matter of seconds before poking his head back into Penny's room, "I told you I'd return, but Nurse Ratched won't let me back in until you're checked out."

The nurse snaps, "Get out."

Penny offers Ted a little smile before he leaves.

When he is allowed back in, she is drifting off to sleep. He kisses her on the head, then takes his seat and her hand.

Fred stops by the ICU after an eventful day. He is happily allowed into Penny's room. He taps Ted on the shoulder, "I heard Penny wakes from time to time."

As if on cue, Penny opens her eyes, and when they find Fred, big tears pop and begin sliding down her cheeks. The detective turns to leave then stops when she says, "Stay."

Penny's eyes practically drill into Fred. Ted gets up from the chair, and Fred fills it. He leans close, "What's bothering you, Penny?"

"Chip's," she whispers.

"Chip's, the diner?"

Penny nods as a few more tears fall.

"Was it someone from Chip's who hurt you?" He takes her hand in his.

Penny nods, "Think so," she barely ekes out.

"Who?"

"Boston."

Let's recap.

The men stay silent until Penny falls back to sleep. Fred motions for Ted to follow him outside her room to an empty waiting area where Fred fills Ted in on recent events.

“I went to see Brenna Campbell; she's the moving consultant whose business card was on the legal pad in Abigail's kitchen. I'll give you a rundown in a minute. Bottom-line: Brenna said a guy named Boston was at Abigail's the day of the murder, and the woman down the hall fighting for her life said Boston shot her."

“Meanwhile, Mike did a trudge through the woods surrounding Granger Mitchell's Carriage House. He found a marked trail leading from a neighboring street to the murder scene. I'll give more of a rundown in a minute.”

Fred takes out his cell, “Mike, I'm at the hospital with Ted. Who's at 275?”

“Everyone.”

“Go ahead and put me on speaker.”

"You're on, Fred."

“Okay, listen up. The good news is that Penny is waking up from time to time.” A loud round of clapping and whooping comes from 275. Fred waits it out. “I'm gonna talk—no interruptions, people. The last time Penny was awake she became very upset. She said that a guy from Chip's diner is the one who hurt her. She said his name is Boston. I already filled some of you in on my conversation with Brenna Campbell; for the rest of you, she's the moving consultant whose business card was on the legal pad in Abigail's kitchen. She said that a Bradley Cooper hunk was leaving Abigail's when she arrived for an appointment. She said he got a phone call and answered it with the word, Boston.

"This is where we are right now. We've got two women mentioning a guy named Boston. One of those women places him at Abigail's condo the day of her murder, the other woman thinks Boston shot her. Mike thinks the murderer is ex-military. I'm gonna run this, so listen up.

"An ex-military guy reconned Abigail's place, got her security codes and keys, went into the condo, did the panty-stuffing-duct-taping-strangulation thing and left. The same ex-military guy trekked through Granger's woods, and with intentional or unintentional help of unlocked doors and an inactivated security system, he got inside the Carriage House for another panty-stuffing-duct-taping-strangulation thing. Strictly speaking, we can look at the strangulation part of the murders as personal preference of a serial killer, but the whole panty-stuffing-duct-taping part is a strong indication that a message was being sent that the victims should have kept their mouths shut."

"Fred, it's Gretchen. Sorry for the interruption, but does this killer think he's the Boston Strangler?"

"Not sure, but serial killers have their preferred way of carrying out a hit. Our guy had success with the strangulation kills, but not with the sniper attempt, so let's run the killer through the filter of Penny's shooting. The same military guy reconned Penny's place, hunkered down until the time was right, and took a kill shot. First question for me is why didn't he keep to his murder script?"

Ted bumps in, "Penny's ex-military. She can probably give as good as she gets. Maybe the killer didn't want to chance that she might get the upper hand."

Mike bumps in, "Our recon killer would know about her military background, so Ted's probably right. His first preference is hand-to-hand combat; that's where he finds success. His second preference is weaponry; that's where he shows weakness."

The team is chomping at the bit to start adding to the discussion, but Fred pulls them up short one more time. "There's one last thing I want to discuss before you guys add on. Penny Meehan just became the most important part of this investigation. While none of us wants to think of her as a loose end, that is exactly what she is—especially now that she survived an assassination attempt. The question that begs asking is—why was Penny a target in the first place?"

The team unloads like rapid fire.

"Penny threw in with Abigail…"

"… and Abigail knew too much about Benton Brettenvue…"

"…and Antonio Alvarez…"

"…and maybe Turner Rodgers…"

"…maybe someone was counting on her to get Topher Griffin in the Governor's seat…"

"…maybe she knew stuff about Celia Brettenvue…"

"…who was also killed…"

"…right before she was scheduled to meet with Dominique at the penitentiary…"

"…who had tons of information about The Realm and Tango."

Fred takes control with a hearty laugh, "Based on **all** of that, the killings of Abigail, Celia, and Dominique make sense: They knew too much to stay alive. I think it's safe to say that Penny Meehan became a target because she found something when she was snooping. The $64 million question is this: What did Penny uncover? That's what we want to know, folks. A final note: After Penny's shooting, I had The Kid research her. Biggest find is that she's Army Reserves, she's thirty-two-years old, came from nothing, joined the Army, and used her military assistance to get a master's degree in journalism from Penn State. A few days ago, this woman got shot, coded in the ER, underwent life-saving emergency surgery, and spent a couple days in an unconscious state. A few minutes ago, she opened her eyes and the first thing she said was that some guy named Boston might be the person who shot her. It would appear the trained reservist and investigative reporter has been working this story even though she's been out of it. Assignments, folks. Ted get what you can from Penny. Find out why she is tying a guy at a luncheonette to her shooting."

He nods. "I'll be with Penny. Stop by before you head out."

Fred addresses the folks at 275. "Mike, I want you to work with Leavy on trying to find out who Boston is."

Mike pushes in. "Fred, we've got the military angle, but Leavy and I should check the survivalist angle, and survivalist groups with ex-military members."

"Good. Randy, forget diving on Abigail's blocks for now. Concentrate your efforts on the two FBI agents who were supposedly guarding Celia Brettenvue the night she was killed."

Manuel pushes in. "Fred, Randy should dovetail that with a review of activity logs from Granger's security provider. We need to know if the Feds left the Carriage House unlocked every night of their protective duty or only on the night of the murder."

"Good. Manuel, research strangulation killings on a countrywide basis. Now that we have the panties and duct tape components, other killings might flag as belonging to this serial killer. The kill order on our victims came from someone very well connected, so whoever hired a contract killer at this level is gonna hire the best in the business. That suggests this isn't Boston's first dog and pony show. That's all for now. I'm gonna stop in to check on Penny one more time, then I'll be back at 275."

Fred stops by, but he doesn't disturb the man who is falling fast for the woman who's fighting to right herself.

Beyond hot and handsome.

Fred steps off the elevator at 275 and heads to the game room where he finds Malcolm and Gretchen waiting for him. He gets right to the point. "The Penny Meehan part of this case is gonna be in your face for a while. I can handle it off-site if it's pressing a sore spot for you two."

Malcolm pushes off the wall he's riding "I'm good, Fred."

Gretchen pushes herself from her seat, "I'm good, too, Fred."

Mike and Leavy pass Mr. and Mrs. Mayor on their way out. "Hey, Fred, can you call Brenna Campbell and get a better description of the Cooper lookalike?"

"Hi, Brenna, it's Fred Serpico."

"What can I do for you, Detective?"

"I was wondering if you could give me some details about Boston beyond 'hot and handsome.'"

"There's nothing beyond hot and handsome, Detective."

Leavy cracks up laughing.

Fred scowls, "Sorry about that, Brenna, I should have told you that you were on speaker phone."

"No problem," she chuckles. "As for Boston, if that's his name, he's probably 40 years old, has medium brown hair and brown eyes. He wore jeans, loafers, and a button-down shirt, cuffed back to mid-forearm. He had a tattoo in that area, but almost all of it was covered by his sleeve."

"Any accent?" Fred asks.

"None that I heard."

"Thanks, Brenna."

"Anytime, Detective."

Mike and Fred head to the kitchen, Leavy heads to the Diving Center. Within minutes she's hacked into governmental data systems at the NARA, MPRC, and DOD, and extracted information on 30-45 year old servicemen and reservists. While she waits for results, she builds a program to isolate individuals with advanced sniper training, or who served in special ops. While that program is running she checks in on Randy.

"Did you get anything on the security angle?"

He nods. "Granger's security provider said the Carriage House had active security on every night of Celia's stay, except for the night of the murder. According to Faye Mitchell, motion detectors at the rear of the estate weren't working that night. She said she mentioned it to the FBI agent who came to inform them about the murder. I've been trying to get information on the two agents on duty that night, but I'm getting cop-blocked. Since I'm still diving in the shallow end of the pool, you're gonna have to tap into the Philly FBI field office system."

"No more kiddie pool for you, Randy. Go into the system, get what you need, and get out."

Manuel joins Leavy at Randy's terminal. They watch as he goes in, gets what he needs, and gets out. Leavy swells with pride, "Our boy's growing up so fast."

Manuel nudges Leavy then heads to his workstation, "I'm gonna get to work on our very own Boston Strangler." He starts by calling Joy Fiancetti at RFI, "Hey, Joy. I need something from the FBI systems, but I've been put on notice by Stacy to stay off the radar."

"No problem. What do you need?"

"Strangulation deaths that have a contract killer or serial killer bent to them."

"Location?"

"Nationwide. I need dates, times, and the names of the local investigators handling the cases. Dive into the files and flag any kinky shit, like panty-stuffing and duct-taping."

"Manuel, I'm married to your father. Panty-stuffing and duct-taping is not considered kinky bedroom antics."

"Could have lived a long happy life without knowing that, Mrs. Fiancetti."

Joy laughs big.

"You about done?" Manuel asks.

"Yup."

"What's the status on John?" he wades in.

"He's staying with RFI for the time being, anyway. He's focusing on work, which is what he does when there's woman trouble. He'll be fine. How are you and Leavy?"

"No words for how good we are. Hey, Joy, did you know what everyone else seems to have known, about Leavy and me?"

Joy laughs, "Your father and I placed bets on how long it would take for you two to acknowledge your feelings."

"Yeah? Who won the bet?"

Joy laughs again, "Well, there were variables that affected our guesses. Like you were involved with Dominique, the psychopath who wanted world domination. Then there was the whole Muriel needed sheltering from her rabid readers. Overall, I'd say you and Leavy are the winners because you finally figured out your shit."

"Yeah. One more thing—the most important thing—how is Charlotte?"

"She's wonderful. Right now she's with Rocco. He's reading her a bedtime story."

"Yeah? What's he reading her?"

"The New York Times."

Stepmother and stepson bust a gut.

Off the grid.

Fred knuckle-wraps the window at Chip's on West Street early the next morning. The eatery is a luncheon-only establishment, so Fred catches the owner before his day gets away from him.

The man of about forty swings the door wide and starts, "I saw you in here with Penny and Captain Johnson. I hope you're here to tell me she's gonna make it."

Fred smiles wide and slaps the man on his shoulder, "It was touch and go, man, but she's fighting her way through."

Chip extends his hand, "Chip Ouellette, come on in. I'll get you some coffee."

"Thanks. Fred Serpico with—"

"RFI. I recognized you when you first came in. I asked Penny why you were in Lewisburg."

"Yeah? What'd she say?"

"She wasn't sure, but she'd find out."

Fred laughs big, "No doubt about that. Penny knows her shit about investigative reporting."

Chip shakes his head, "Always told her she was gonna poke her nose somewhere it didn't belong."

"You think that's what happened here?"

Chip shrugs, "Not sure, but when you start poking the bear, it's not gonna waste its time growling, it's gonna kill you."

Fred nods, drains his coffee and eagerly accepts another. "So Chip, Penny linked her shooter to your diner. Any idea why?"

"I doubt she thinks it's one of my regulars. My place seats forty-eight people Fred, and all forty-eight seats are filled every day with lunch regulars. I'm guessing Penny suspects her shooter was the new guy who came in the day she was shot."

Fred remains silent.

Chip fills the silence.

"This guy eyed Penny a bit and when he realized she was eyeing him back, he came to the counter and introduced himself. He said he was staring at her because she looked familiar, and maybe he knew her from being in the military."

Chip is giving Fred everything he needs, so the detective simply nods and sips his black and white.

"Anyway, the guy introduced himself as Paul Boston, said he's 'Marine through and through.' Penny introduced herself as, Staff Sergeant SSG Penelope Meehan, Army Reserves. She suggested he try the chicken parmesan salad on garlic bread and went back to her Cobb salad. Not much else was said between the two. The guy waited until Penny was back at *Kiss and Tell* before he headed out."

"He get into a car?"

"A beautiful blue Jag," Chip smiles.

"Yeah? Any chance you saw the plates?"

"Sorry, man."

Fred finishes his second coffee and puts his hand over the top when Chip goes to refill it. "So tell me Chip, do you think the Jag driving Marine might be Penny's shooter?"

The man shrugs his shoulders, "I can't say one way or the other, but I tend not to question Penny. If she says he's the shooter, he's the shooter. Penny's got a nose for these things, Fred, but I sure do wish she didn't go sticking it where it doesn't belong, you know?"

Fred knows.

Philly

Fred spends the next week sequestered at the Carriage House on Old Estate Road. He walks the grounds, follows the yellow tape trail into the woods, spends a night on the floor of the room where Celia's body was found. But mostly, he spends his time pouring over notes Granger made during his weekly meetings with Dominique at the penitentiary, and the ones Granger and McKay Wallace made during their interview sessions with Celia.

"There's plenty of threads to pull on the things Mrs. Brettenvue had to say about her husband's involvement with the Peruvian crime lord and the project known as Tango, but her knowledge was mostly based on snooping and eavesdropping. Dominique, on the other hand was all-in with The Realm and one of its leaders, and she'd been giving Granger bits and pieces for months." Fred starts his review, catalogs a few bits and pieces, then compares them to The Octopus summary Stacy Remington made. He does this each day, and on the last he reviews his body of work and rereads the summary.

"Organizational structure, The Body, and 8 ancillary leaders: 6 from South America, 1 from Africa, 1 from the U.S." He spends a few minutes at the wall of windows staring out at the heavy tree line then talks some things through, "Roland Gaffney was arrested because of his involvement with The Realm. That left his leadership position open. Dominique Brettenvue was vying for a position in the organization, but..." He moves to the window at the front of the estate, folds his arms across his chest, spreads his legs, and locks his knees—a very good indication that he's in for the long haul of processing. He reads through the summary again, this time concentrating on the countries of origin of the men Dominique gave up, "Peru, Africa, Argentina, Chile, Brazil, Guatemala, Columbia." He makes his way to the kitchen for a cup of coffee, his fifth of the day. While the pot perks, he gets lost in a conversation Peyton and Ted had…

"I told you that the Tango had influences from the German Waltz, Czech Polka, Polish Mazurka, Bohemian Schottische, Cuban Habanera, African Candombe and the Argentinian Milonga."

"G, C, P, B, C, A, A," Ted said.

Peyton squealed, "Yes! You get it!"

"It's obvious."

"Cool. So it jumps out at you, too?"

Ted smiled.

Manuel pushed in, "Would one of you care to share what the hell you're talking about?"

"German, Czech, Polish, Bohemian, Cuban, African, and Argentinian," Peyton said.

"G, C, P, B, C, A, A," Ted said.

"Guatemala, Columbia, Peru, Brazil, Chile, Africa, and Argentina," Peyton and Ted said in unison. Ted finished it up for the others, "Seven of the eight Realm leaders, or supposed leaders, come from countries that begin with the letter of the countries that developed the Tango. Suggesting coincidence is a factor in these countries, these initials, and these individuals being involved in The Realm and Tango falls far outside the parameters of reasonability."

"Far, far outside," Peyton chimed in.

Ted continued. "In the overall scheme of things this information may not be worth much to our murder investigations, but it presents solid evidence that the name of the dance is integral to the impetus of The Realm."

"Integral to the impetus of the organization? Or integral to a specific program or arm of The Octopus? What if the people Dominique gave up weren't the leaders? What if they were part of Tango and nothing else? What if there are seven other arms working seven other programs for The Body? What if Alvarez and the others are program leaders, and there are eight echelon leaders working directly with or for The Body?"

He takes a few minutes at the back windows with his black and white. He is still standing there, when – the – penny – drops. "If Dominique gave up a bunch of lower level program leaders, and she kept the real leaders' names secret, that would definitely be enough to get her killed."

Fred takes one more pass through Dominique's file and hits paydirt—a notation made by Granger and underlined several times. Fred reads it out loud, "Dominique confirmed that The Realm wanted control over the vast intelligence realm known as cyberland. To accomplish this goal, they would kidnap, hold, and weaponize the top ranked cyber huntress, Joy Ann Watts, now known as, Joy Fiancetti. When they were unable to get her, they went after the second ranked huntress, Annie Mahoney-Maxwell."

The next entry Granger Mitchell made pulls Fred up short. He notices the shake of his hand holding the paper. He croaks out the words. "The kidnapping of FICA Agent, Hannah Leavy, was significant beyond the kidnapping itself..." Fred rummages through the files looking for more, there is no more. "Significant, how? How? Goddammit, how?"

Fred makes a mental note to pull Leavy's kidnapping case and review the hell out of it. He leaves the Carriage House carrying a box full of information on Celia Brettenvue, puts the box into Janelle's Jeep and heads to Ted Brothers' place. His help is needed to get the place ready for a very important house guest.

It's him, 100% him.

Ted Brothers drives his Land Rover onto the driveway, then onto the front lawn, parking it as close to the front door as possible. He is followed by Captain Johnson and his wife. As soon as the vehicle doors open, Wanda takes immediate control. She leans into the Land Rover, says a few words to Penny, who nods her head. The men step back, at the ready, but they let Wanda and Penny work things out.

Fred and Mike are already inside and have already rearranged Ted's den for the first stage of Penny's recuperation. Drawing on his own experience with a GSW shoulder injury, Mike suggested that Penny camp out on a recliner for the foreseeable future. The men set the recliners side by side, one for the patient, one for the person attending her, and put an end table between the two. They brought a small dresser down from upstairs and set about filling it with things the women at 275 sent; T-shirts, tank tops, leggings, sweatpants, undergarments, socks, nightgowns, and a silky coral-colored bathrobe that Gretchen and Leavy included for when Penny feels better. On the top of the dresser, the men set a basket full of all sorts of body lotions, hand creams, fluffy slippers, and magazines, a gift from Mr. and Mrs. Damian

Johnson. They also stocked the kitchen with every conceivable thing Penny could ever crave, as well as a homemade chicken soup prepared by Gretchen and Malcolm, with a lovely note expressing their happiness that Penny is on the road to recovery.

By the time Wanda gets Penny onto one of the recliners and checks her dressings and vitals, Penny is wiped out. She struggles to thank Wanda and Damian for their help before drifting off. Physician Assistant Johnson takes control again by going over the discharge papers and prescription schedule with Ted before leaving. She points to the set of stairs just off the den, "That woman is not to step foot on those stairs. Understood?"

"Yes, ma'am," Ted accepts the order and the hug she gives.

Fred and Mike have chicken soup with Ted then have a little welcome home party when Penny wakes an hour later. The patient's celebration consists of prescription pills and orange juice. When she's comfortable again, Fred sits next to her. Ted and Mike fill the space across the room at the entrance to Ted's home office.

"Can I get you anything, Penny?"

"I'm good, Fred," she fakes.

"No, not yet, but you're getting there," he smiles. "Mike and I will be leaving soon, so you can get a good night's sleep, but I'd like you to tell me what you told Ted about Boston, if you're able."

Penny nods, then struggles through, "I got a sketchy vibe from him from the get-go. He said he thought he recognized me because I look military. I introduced myself as Staff Sergeant SSG Penelope Meehan, Army Reserves, he said he was Paul Boston, Marine through and through." She's already shaking her head when her good hand gets into the action squeezing her pantleg. "My red flag first went up when he didn't introduce himself with his rank—it started waving full-out as our meeting continued. I've been Army Reserves for years and have been around Army men long enough to know one when I see one—my gut was telling me that Paul Boston **was not** Marines. My gut was proven right when he reached across the lunch counter for his soda, and I saw two yellow trimmed points of a tattoo peeking out from under his cuffed-back button-down shirt. The points are unmistakably part of an Army star tattoo. I have that same tattoo, so I'm 100% sure he's Army, and not Marines."

Fred offers her a Serpico smile and encourages her on, "You're doing great, Penny. Continue, unless you need a break."

She continues. "As for the shooting, I'd been home for a couple hours, had taken a shower, had straightened the place, and was on my couch reading and waiting for Ted. I was having trouble concentrating. I had a feeling something wasn't right with my place. No matter how hard I tried to concentrate, I just couldn't shake the feeling. Then something caught my eye at the front window—a flash—a movement—a reflection from behind—I don't know what, but I had a split-second thought that must have registered in me as fear, because I started a right-hand dive onto the couch. I know there wasn't much time between the instinct to dive and my being shot, but in that space of time I knew the shooter was the guy from the diner."

Fred gets off his seat and moves to Penny. He kneels in front of her and takes her unslung hand in his, "Staff Sergeant Penelope Meehan, you are a fine soldier and a remarkable woman. I am happy to know you." He kisses the top of her head, places his hand there for a minute then heads to Mike and Ted. He shakes Ted's hand, "You two need anything, call us. Mr. and Mrs. Mayor are putting us up in an empty apartment at 275 for the duration, but we'll be back to spend time with Penny whenever you need or want us."

They turn to say goodbye to Penny, but she's already drifted off.

275

There's an energy when Fred and Mike arrive at the penthouse.

"What's going on?" they ask in unison.

Leavy is practically jumping out of her skin, “Mike you are a genius! I added a segment into my program that isolated former servicemen who are involved with survivalist groups—there are thousands by the way—but I got a hit.” She hands her laptop to Mike

“Holy fuck!” he says as he eyes the face that could belong to Bradley Cooper. He reads the name below the picture, “Paul Ferraro.”

After Fred takes a look at the Cooper doppelganger, Leavy fills them in on her findings, “If that man is our contract killer, he is former Army Ranger, Master Sergeant, Paul Ferraro. He lives in Chevy Chase, Maryland, and is owner of twelve U.S. based survivalist training schools called, Intestinal Fortitude. Those words are an important component of the Ranger’s Creed.”

“Good job Leavy. Can you send this to Ted Brothers right now, let’s see if Penny IDs Paul Ferraro as the guy from the diner?”

“On its way, Fred.”

Drexel Hill

Ted opens the text from Leavy and increases the size of the picture. He hands his phone to Penny, “Is this Boston?”

Penny nods before she answers, “It’s him, 100% it’s him.”

From Ted: It's him, 100% it's him.
From Fred: Kiss our girl goodnight.
From Ted: With pleasure.

Penny lowers the recliner that she's been perched upon, "Ted, since I'm awake, I think I'll hit the head." He helps her to the bathroom, then goes to the kitchen to heat some soup. When she returns, he offers to bring her meal to the recliner.

"I'd rather sit at the table."

He starts to help her.

"I'm good, Ted." She struggles getting in place. Her left shoulder is wrapped tight with her left arm bent across her chest. The whole wrapping thing is supported by a sling.

"You know, Penny, I'm here to help."

Penny nods at the handsome man with the most beautiful green eyes she's ever seen, "I know you are, and I'm really very grateful that you took me in, but you barely know me, and you've already done so much. Why are you letting me stay here with you, Ted?"

"Honestly, Penny, I don't exactly know. At the risk of sounding weird, I felt a little thing for you when we met, and I haven't been able to walk away."

Penny smiles. "I felt a little thing for you, that's why I flirted. But if we'd had our date the other night I was going to tell you that I don't get involved with married men," Penny's eyes travel to Ted's wedding ring. "The fact that you stayed by my side at the hospital and invited me here suggests maybe you aren't married."

Ted shakes his head, "Widowed."

Pain etches Penny's face, "I'm sorry, Ted. At the risk of sounding like an intrusive reporter, when did you lose your wife?"

"Janelle. She was killed in a mall shooting three years ago."

"The Track Mall Massacre?"

He cringes at the name. "Yes."

"Your wife was shot?" she ekes.

Ted nods. He catches the *something* that travels Penny's face—it unsettles him, makes him defend his actions. "I'm not taking care of you because I couldn't take care of Janelle." Ted reaches across the table and takes Penny's unslung fisted hand, "I'm taking care of you because it feels right."

Penny's fist slowly relaxes. She twines their fingers together, "I've never had anyone take care of me before. It feels very strange, but very wonderful." She pulls a long, deep breath, "Ted, would you mind taking care of me by helping me to the recliner? I'm afraid I'm about to pass out."

275

It's all-hands-on-deck in the Diving Center. Those with cyber skills are researching the hell out of Paul Ferraro; the others are waiting for a formal update. Leavy does the honors, "Paul Ferraro, better known as our contract killer, Paul Boston, is a forty-four-year old, highly decorated former Army Ranger. He and his wife, Felicity Ferraro, a well-established defense attorney in DC, live in an exclusive area of Chevy Chase, Maryland, with their four young children. He is majority owner of twelve Intestinal Fortitude training schools located across the country. The three closest facilities are located in Georgia, Maryland, and New York. We've got him on security feeds on I-95 points north and south between Chevy Chase and Philadelphia on several occasions, and on I-476 points north and south, to Lewisburg and Scranton."

The team starts gnawing at that bone—the Mayor, on the other hand, starts eyeing his wife from across the room. He concerns about the exhaustion on her face and approaches her with extended hand, "Come on Woman, I'm taking you two to bed." When Gretchen doesn't raise an objection, a ping of concern pongs through the man. "Gretchen, are you feeling okay?"

She nods, "I've just hit a wall, I think."

Malcolm escorts his wobbly wife to their bedroom and waits while she gets ready for bed. He tucks in Mommy, and her perfectly round baby ball, with a kiss to the forehead and one to the belly, "Do you want me to stay until you're asleep?"

Gretchen is too tired to answer, she simply shakes her head once and drifts off.

The plan involves a whole lot of lying.

Fred is up before dawn. He has parked his butt on the couch overlooking a softly illuminated and somewhat eerily empty, Hufnagle Park. He is processing, and texting, and calling, and getting others up before dawn.

Fred: Very sorry for early text. Is this the man with Abigail that day?
Brenna: It's him. 100%.
Fred: Any idea what kind of car he drove?
Brenna: Beautiful blue sports car.
Fred: Thank you.
Brenna: You're welcome.

~

Fred: I need to know what kind of car was parked near Penny's condo.
Mike: Blue Jaguar. You could have just knocked on my door.

~

Fred: Get your ass up and come to the great room.
Manuel: Do you own a clock?
Fred: Yeah. It says it's half-past when I kick your ass.
Manuel: Those were John Maxwell's last words.

Fred calls Chip's landline on West Street. "I need your cell number. I'm gonna send a picture for an ID ..... great, thanks."

Fred: Is this Boston?
Chip: Yup. 100%.

Fred calls his boss, “Rocco, the team has what they need on Paul Ferraro, aka Boston. I’m gonna run it for you.”

“Si. Proceed.”

“The suspect was placed at Abigail’s condo on the day of her murder by a moving consultant who was inside the unit that day. The suspect was placed at a luncheonette early on the day of Penny’s shooting by the shooting victim and by the owner of the eatery. A blue Jag, also ID’d as a blue sports car, was present at three locations associated with the murders and the shooting. Paul Ferraro owns a blue Jaguar F-Type. The suspect is a trained military expert in hand-to-hand combat and an expert sniper. Abigail and Celia were murdered by strangulation; Penny’s assassination attempt was made with an assault rifle. The suspect is a trained survivalist, which connects him to the tree trudging and trail markings at Granger Mitchell’s property. We have camera tracking of him driving through the state of Pennsylvania with multiple stops in Philadelphia, Lewisburg, and Scranton within the time frames of Abigail’s and Celia’s deaths and Penny’s shooting. We want to move this forward.”

“Si. Advise.”

"RFI is on a no-communication directive with Stacy Remington. As soon as we hang up, I'm gonna reach out to Granger Mitchell and have him contact the director, who in turn will contact Manuel, who will tell her about our plan."

"Keep me looping in your plan."

Fred hangs up—places a call—enacts a plan.

Philly

Granger Mitchell answers the very early phone call from Fred Serpico. As requested, he disconnects from that call–places a call–initiates a plan. The plan involves a whole lot of lying. "Sorry for the early hour, Stacy."

"Granger, is all well?"

"Yes, yes. This call is not of a personal nature. It concerns the Celia Brettenvue murder. Are you at liberty to discuss this issue?"

"I'm at home, still, it's best to be brief."

"Very well. I was reviewing the Celia Brettenvue files at the Carriage House, and I've found something. A name. I was reviewing my handwritten notations, and I remembered Celia saying the authorities should focus their attention on this person, and if they pulled the right threads they would find a connection to Tango and The Realm. I pulled Dominique's files, and I found a similar notation. The name is causing me consternation, Stacy."

“That’s enough, Granger. I’ll call you back from a secure line.” When she does, she is instructed to call Manuel.

275

Manuel joins Fred at the bank of windows.

Fred starts right in, “I got the go-ahead on Boston from Rocco. I called Granger and put the wheels in motion on our plan. He’s going to link you up with Director Remington. Let me know when you’re done with that conversation. I’ll be with Malcolm. When Mr. Mayor hears what’s going on, he might kick our asses out of 275.”

Fred sends another wakeup text.

Fred: We need to talk. Without Gretchen. Your office.
Malcolm: On my way.

Give or take 1%, ma'am.

"Former Agent Xavier, this is Director Remington."

"Good morning, ma'am. What is the status on your communication, ma'am?"

"Secure line."

"Very well, ma'am. RFI is ready to make an arrest in the Abigail Forrester and Celia Brettenvue murders, and the attempted murder of Penny Meehan."

"Who is your suspect?"

"Paul Ferraro, a highly decorated former Army Ranger—"

"I know who Paul Ferraro is. I know his wife, Felicity Ferraro, as well. She's an attorney at the law firm, Preston and Porter. Her clientele is exclusive to some heavy hitters in DC, including Senator Turner Rodgers. You'd better be sure, Manuel."

"We're 99% sure, give or take 1%, ma'am."

"If I had a penny."

"Ma'am?"

"Your standard reply, Xavier, 99% sure."

"Yes, ma'am."

"Continue. What is your plan?"

"RFI can arrest Paul Ferraro outright, or you can be in on it. That's your call, ma'am. The arrest can be made at his home in Chevy Chase,

Maryland, although there's no telling what events will unfold. He has a wife and four young children who live with him, so we would prefer to make the arrest elsewhere. Since he works from home and his businesses are spread across the country, we would rather arrest him in Philadelphia, the state of this crimes."

"Is Mr. Ferraro expected back in Philadelphia?"

"We believe so, ma'am. We initiated a plan to lure him to the Granger Mitchell property on Old Estate Road. When Granger called you this morning, he put our plan into motion. I'm assuming you know there isn't a name in Celia's files that connects Tango to The Realm, or if there is, we've yet to find it."

"Yes, Manuel, I figured that one out."

"Of course, ma'am. It's my understanding that you've been working from home, Director."

"Yes."

"Surveillance issues at J. Edgar, ma'am?"

"Yes."

"And at your home?"

"I've been scanning daily. Thus far, I'm keeping ahead of unwanted ears. I admit I didn't scan this morning before my conversation with Granger."

"We were counting on that ma'am. John Maxwell tapped into your phone this morning. Others were already tapped in, ma'am. Your conversation with Granger was overheard. We suspect the information has been shared with the appropriate people within The Realm. Before we proceed further, what is your current communication status?"

"Secure line."

"Yes, ma'am. Maxwell just confirmed that. As I was saying, ma'am, we have a plan to get Paul Ferraro to come to us."

"Tell me about the plan."

Chevy Chase

The phone rings early in the stately home of Paul and Felicity Ferraro. It is her phone that's caused the disturbance, so she answers it, "Irish."

"There's a problem."

She remains silent.

"Stacy Remington received a call from Granger Mitchell this morning. He found something in the Celia Brettenvue notes—a name that connects Tango to The Realm. Apparently, the name causes Mitchell consternation. The FICA Director is booked on a flight to Philly tonight. She is meeting Attorney Mitchell at his Cottage on Old Estate Road. Remington cannot learn that name. Have the hit done first, then get the files. No mistakes. This has to be a clean hit."

Felicity is out of bed before the call is disconnected. Paul is not too far behind. She begins pacing the room. He knows what she's thinking.

"Don't you even think about calling him to do this hit, Felicity. This one is mine."

She snarls. "You screwed up the Penny Meehan hit, Paul. You're rusty."

He repeats his words. "This is **my** hit, Felicity. I will take care of this." He takes her phone from her hand just as there is a tiny knock on their bedroom door, "Mommy. Daddy. May we come in?"

275

Malcolm returns to the master bedroom from his meeting with Fred. He kisses Gretchen on the cheek, "Woman, I'm sorry to wake you, but RFI is making a move to arrest Boston that you need to know about."

"You're not involved, are you?"

Malcolm lifts his wife's wrist and places his fingers onto her pulse point, it immediately picks up speed. "Woman, you need to slow your roll or I'm going to insist that you be kept in the dark."

She nods.

He continues. "I'm not involved."

"Randy?" she asks.

"Granger," he answers.

Gretchen throws back the bedcovers, "Nope. Absolutely. Not. Going. To. Happen." She puts her hand out for a hoist.

Malcolm ignores it, "Woman."

"Don't Woman me, Malcolm Price." He offers her his hand. She swats it away and stays put.

"Gretchen, stop," he growls.

Rage tears fill her eyes. She calls beyond her husband, "Manuel Xavier, get your ass in here, now!"

Fred follows Manuel into the room, "I'm here as backup." He takes one look at Gretchen and adds, "or as a prosecution witness, depending greatly on how things play out."

"Good, the troublesome-twosome. Listen up, do whatever it is you need to do to get the bad guys, but keep my father out of it. Is that clear?"

Gretchen is silenced by the shock of seeing Granger Mitchell filling the doorway, "Gretchen Rae Mitchell, **that** is enough."

"Daddy? When did you get here?"

"We arrived recently."

"We?"

Just then an arm and a waving hand appears from around her father's back, "Good morning, Gretchen," Faye says.

"Oh, good Lord, you're all in on it. Well, I forbid it, and that's the end of the discussion. If the RFI men and women want to go after the bad guys, I say Godspeed and please be careful, but they will not take my sixty-five-year-old father with them on their James Bond escapades. And Faye, I'd expect better of you. What on earth are you thinking letting Daddy entertain this nonsense?"

"Out!" Granger bellows. "Everyone but the father of my unborn granddaughter, please leave this room, now."

A mini stampede bottlenecks the doorway as Manuel, Fred, and Faye scramble to get out. Gretchen hoists herself from her bed, and storms past her father and husband, "Since neither of you felt the need to include me **before** the life and death decisions were made, there is no need to include me now." She continues to the en suite and locks the door behind her.

Malcolm is waiting in the bedroom for his wife to emerge from the shower. She addresses him with a flattened edge of anger in her voice, "If you are concerned with upsetting me, then I suggest you leave."

"Gretchen, please talk to me."

"Please leave."

Malcolm storms from the room in search of Manuel, "This fucking plan of yours better end with Granger Mitchell in one piece," he says before storming to his office and slamming his door.

Steve should take the shot.

Most of the RFI team heads out of 275 for different reasons and for different destinations.

Mike drives Leavy to Philadelphia so she can provide protection to Penny while Ted is with the RFI team at Old Estate Road. Mike fills the Philly detective in on the specifics of the plan, then spends time with Penny and Leavy, while Ted gets his gear ready.

Fred heads to the airport to meet the RFI jet. He greets his former MFPD partner, Steve Phelps, with a w.i.d.e. Serpico smile, "Damned good to see you, Steve." He helps load some gear into Janelle's Jeep, then heads to the Granger Mitchell estate.

Steve listens intently to the plan, asks a few questions, runs the logistics through his head, and opines, "We don't need the Director on-site. All we need to do is get Granger in place, let Boston set for his shot, and I'll take Boston out. Stacy Remington does not need to be inside."

"Remington doesn't want this to be an RFI only operation. With her there, we have an FBI witness. With Ted Brothers there, we have a Philly PD witness. And with Granger Mitchell there, we have our legal asses covered."

"Your call."

"Manuel's call."

"Noted. When do I meet up with Mike?"

"Half-hour." Fred places a call, "Head over to Old Estate Road."

Drexel Hill

Mike hangs up from Fred, "Ted, we leave in five minutes. Hey, Leavy, let's do a perimeter check."

Ted grabs his gear, puts it at the front door, then goes in to be with Penny—he finds she's wound pretty tight. He moves in front of her chair, "How you doing?"

She starts to say something, then thinks better of it.

He extends his hand, "Do you think you can sit with me on the couch for a minute or two?"

She lowers her chair and lets Ted help her up and then to the couch. After she is settled, he sits to the right of her, "Lean in to me."

Penny nestles her good side deeply into Ted, he stretches his arm across the back of the couch, careful not to rest it on her body. "Pretend I'm holding you tight." He kisses the top of her head. "I need you to relax and take care of yourself. If I know you're okay, I'll be able to focus on the plan. Can you do that, Penny?"

She nods, then pulls free from his pretend-embrace. She fights the tears that threaten as he helps her up. She turns to him, "Hug me or hold me—whatever we can do before you go."

Ted opens his arms wide, Penny steps into them, he wraps them gently around her. He r.e.s.p.o.n.d.s. to the woman's press against him. "Damn, Penny, there's no way in hell I'm not coming back to you. We have unfinished business."

Penny sighs, and when Ted kisses her deeply, all her girly bits beg for his attention.

Ted Brothers walks away, taking their desire with him.

275

Manuel stayed back at the penthouse reviewing the plan with Granger and Malcolm. He answered their questions, and when it came time to fit Granger with Kevlar, shit got heavy.

Malcolm walks to the line of respectability with his father-in-law. "You should not be doing this. Something—everything—about this feels wrong."

Granger places his hand onto Malcolm's shoulder, "Take care of Gretchen and Faye."

Manuel finds a quiet place and runs the plan looking for holes, then gives his father a call. "This is the plan, find the holes: Steve and Mike will be in the woods long before the meeting time of 10 PM. Steve will be set for his shot—Mike will be watching for Ferraro and communicating with Steve—Fred will be with me in the Carriage House—Ted Brothers will be on the first floor of Granger's house. Stacy will arrive at the front door, and Granger will bring her through the house to the kitchen, which is a big room with one wall of windows that overlooks the forested area. Everyone, except Granger, will have audio and voice communication, everyone will have Kevlar, and those who need it will have night vision capability. Work it through, boss."

The head of RFI delivers his words sans his customary kitschy Italian, easily reverting back to former MI6 British Intelligence Officer, Rocco Fiancetti. "No holes on the setup, Son, but I do have thoughts. The hit is the primary objective; file retrieval is secondary. The assassin is highly motivated to make the kill **before** Granger has a chance to tell Stacy anything. Boston will be in his lair waiting for the first opportunity to shoot Attorney Mitchell. He'll want to eliminate his target **before** Stacy even arrives. That's the only way Boston can manage both objectives: silence Granger and get the files. Granger Mitchell needs to stay out of the kitchen, and out of the line of fire until the last possible moment. As for Director Remington, her foremost objective is the protection of Granger, but she has a mole in her organization. She will want Ferraro taken alive so he can lead her to her traitor. Her preferred outcome may not be achievable if we are to keep Granger Mitchell alive."

"Understood."

"As soon as the assassin readies for the shot, Steve should take his."

Gretchen stays behind closed doors until the need for sustenance wins the battle over petulance. Faye leaves the kitchen when Gretchen arrives so father and daughter have privacy. Granger points to a seat, "I'd like you to sit, Gretchen."

She obliges. She remains quiet, watching her father move about making her toast, and pouring her a large glass of iced orange juice. "I hear that my granddaughter is fond of her juice."

Gretchen smiles and touches her baby ball. She nibbles the toast and sips her juice in silence. Her father breaks the silence.

"Gretchen, there are dangers associated with tonight's plan, but there are dangers for me, Faye, McKay, and Randy, already. We know things, or the people involved in Tango and The Realm think we know things. There was a murder on my property, Gretchen. There is no reason to think the killer won't come back at some point, and every reason to think that he will. I am compelled to act. You do not have to agree with my actions, but I request that you support them, nonetheless."

It is at that precise moment DelRae Price begins a flourish of kicks and rolls. Gretchen's eyes fill at the celebration of life within. She goes to her father, takes his hand, and places it on her baby ball. She lets him enjoy her cartwheeling baby, then locks her pleading eyes onto his, "Please Daddy, please do whatever it takes to come back safely. DelRae and I desperately need you."

Granger pulls his girl into his arms and whispers, "I promise."

The Baby Mama takes her usual place on the leather couch overlooking Hufnagle Park while her father goes to spend time with Faye. When it's time for goodbyes, she joins everyone at the elevator and embraces her father and Manuel. She graciously accepts their promises that they will return unharmed.

"Where is Fred?" she asks nervously.

"He went directly from the airport to Old Estate Road."

"Manuel, if time permits, please extend my apologies to Fred and express my desperate need that you all return safely."

When the doors close and the sound of the descending elevator fills the space with dread, Gretchen returns to her bedroom without so much as a word to Malcolm, Faye, or Randy.

I'd better be on the job.

The shit with Felicity hit the fan as soon as the kids got off to school.

"I'm sending Trellis."

"The fuck you are, Felicity."

"I already called him. Put your damned ego aside—an ego that isn't warranted after the fuck up with the tabloid reporter, by the way."

"Fuck, Felicity. Twenty fucking years in rank, thousands of shots, hundreds of missions, and I miss the mark one goddamn time."

"Look, Paul, if the plan were to strangle the life out of tonight's victim, you'd be the only one I'd send. For this assignment, Trellis is a better fit." She answers an incoming call before her very pissed-off husband offers a rebuttal. "Trellis. I thought this was settled ..... I need you in Philadelphia tonight ..... break your plans ..... yeah, he's here..." She hands the phone off to Paul.

"What do you want, Trellis? ..... I'm not the one with the problem ..... she's freaking out because of the Penny Meehan hit ..... I know they came down on her ..... I'm good to go ..... good, don't cancel a fucking thing." He slams the phone onto the kitchen counter, "I'm going to take a shower. When I get back, Felicity, you'd better be off the phone, and I'd better be on the job."

Boston's drive from Chevy Chase to Philly helped smooth out most of the rough edges, but he is still pretty pissed when he enters the woods behind Granger Mitchell's place. He berates himself, "You're losing your fucking edge. Put it —put her—out of your head. Clear your fucking head, Ferraro."

He's halfway through the forested area when he realizes he's been moving on total recall. He stops and orients himself—pulls himself under control, connects with the mission, quiets his advance. "This hit needs to go off without a hitch. This one's been a long time coming." He moves out—moves through—becomes one with his surroundings. He stops his forward momentum several hundred feet from the property line, "Familiar territory," he settles into his place and lets the last time he was there run through his head…

He stepped into the lair he set for himself behind Granger Mitchell's Cottage. From his vantage point he could see the FBI detail parked between the two stone structures. He trained his sights onto the main house, "Let's make sure no one's home. Mr. and Mrs. Mitchell should still be at the mayoral election celebration in Lewisburg, but…" His sights were trained on the place for ten minutes before he gave it an 'all clear'. He waited for the agents to go into and return from the Carriage House after conducting the 8 PM check on Celia Brettenvue, then waited until it was lights out in her bedroom, then waited a few minutes for her to settle in, then waited for the chance to squeeze the life out of her.

He begins his forward move. "That was then; this is now. You're on your own. No one to make sure the sensors are off. Make sure you stay outside the range of security triggers." He finds the lair he used the night he killed Celia. He sets himself in.

Mike locks his infrared scope onto Paul Ferraro when he steps inside the quarter-mile perimeter from the back of the estate. From that point on, Mike doesn't take his eyes off his mark. He and Steve had canvassed the area behind the Cottage and Carriage House when they first arrived, looking for the assassin's fire sight…

"Steve, the killer made his approach to the Celia Brettenvue murder scene through those woods," Mike pointed. "It's a three-quarter mile trail that he's set with reflective tape markers. There's no way he trekked through and went directly into the Carriage House for the killing. He had to have set a surveillance spot somewhere in this area," Mike suggested.

"Like this one?" Steve smiled and pointed.

"Yeah, like that one."

The men surveilled the lair without disturbing it. "From this vantage point, he has a perfect view of the back door, and inside the kitchen of the Cottage, and he has a perfect view into the Carriage House. Fred and Manuel will need to stay low while they wait." Steve scanned the surrounding area, looking for the right place to lie in wait for his target. "There. That tree's perfect." He scanned again and pointed to an area 500 yards in the opposite direction from the killer's lair, "You should set up there. There's a small retaining wall along where the land slopes down. You'll be plenty obscured in the gully. Ferraro might not expect company in the woods, but he's trained military, so he'll be looking. That spot will keep you out of sight."

"He'll have night vision."

"Taking chances here, Mike. Our goal is to 'lure and capture'. We should be prepared to shoot to kill."

The planning and readying is behind them. The RFI shooters are in place and set for action. The backup RFI shooter updates his team, "200 yards from lair." He and Steve train their scopes on the assassin as he settles in, sets his tripod, and secures his rifle.

Steve whispers, "He's mounted."

Boston takes his binoculars and scans the bottom floor of the Cottage, then the upstairs, then the bottom floor again. He lowers his hand a fraction of an inch, turns his head slightly to the left toward Steve, raises the viewers again, and scans the woods; first in Mike's direction, then toward the Carriage House, then back to the Cottage. He puts the binoculars aside, checks the time on his watch, goes flat on his stomach, inches into place, sights through his scope, and waits for visual on his victim.

Mike and Steve go on high alert when they hear Granger greet Stacy.

"Come in, Stacy."

The director enters the Cottage, takes a set of earbuds from Detective Ted Brothers, who is cloaked in shadow at the front entrance of the Mitchell estate. She follows Granger through a magnificent stone, steel, and glass foyer, halts her progression for a fraction-of-a-fraction-of-a-second, reaches out to touch him to stop him, then shakes off whatever IT was that nudged her, and continues on with the ruse.

"You have a name for me. Someone associated with The Realm?" she asks, playing her part, the supposed reason behind her trip from DC to Philly.

"I do."

They made it halfway into the kitchen when they stop. The abrupt halt places Granger in the crosshairs of the assassin lying in wait just beyond a wall of windows. A second, maybe two, passes.

Three shooters in the tree line ready themselves when Stacy Remington and Granger Mitchell enter the kitchen.

Boston sights, then moves his finger to the trigger.

"He's ready for shot…"

The assassin lifts his head a fraction, turns left — And. Pulls. The. Trigger.

"Granger and Stacy down!" Mike yells.

Steve shoots his target and yells, "**Shooter down. MOVE. MOVE. MOVE!"**

Ted charges the kitchen. Fred and Manuel run from the Carriage House to the Cottage. Mike and Steve surround the assassin. Steve does weapons control. Mike checks for vitals. "Call it in, Steve, he's alive."

Within minutes, two on-call ambulances arrive at the Carriage House. One speeds away with a patient. One drives away with a DOA.

There is a casualty.

Malcolm knocks before entering the bedroom. He finds his woman curled into a fetal position staring off into space. He goes and sits on the floor next to her.

"Is it over?"

"Yes."

"Is everyone coming home alive?"

Malcolm wraps his hand around her wrist and feels the thumping of her pulse.

"There is a casualty. Stacy Remington."

Gretchen goes from hopeful, to hysterical, to hyperventilating, in rapid succession. "Oh, poor Stacy. Oh, poor Daddy." She sobs.

Malcolm hops over her onto the bed and pulls her into his arms. "Gretchen, please."

Damian and Wanda knock and enter the bedroom. Wanda approaches the couple. "Gretchen we're going to calm you down with or without drugs; the choice is yours," Wanda says as she starts to put a blood pressure cuff onto Gretchen's arm.

The refusing patient lets out a few racking breaths and takes Wanda's hand, "Don't. I'm done. I'm completely done. You don't need to stay on my account." She pulls herself from

Malcolm's arms, accepts a hoisting-hand from Wanda and leaves the room.

Philadelphia
It is nearly 5 AM when FBI Director Shelby Webber arrives at Pennsylvania Hospital. She wants to go to Stacy Remington. Instead, she goes to the ICU to deal with Paul Ferraro.

"Former Agent Xavier, please update me on the events post-shootings."

"Within a minute of firing his rifle, the shooter of Stacy Remington, Paul Ferraro, was approached by RFI team members, Steve Phelps and Michael Monopoli. Phelps secured the firearm, Monopoli performed triage. No words were spoken to the downed man. RFI team member Fred Serpico arrived at the scene within minutes accompanied by EMTs, who had been on standby. Serpico read Mr. Ferraro his rights as witnessed by five individuals: two paramedics; Specialist Monopoli; RFI sniper, Steve Phelps; and myself. Serpico rode in the ambulance with Mr. Ferraro and remained inside the emergency treatment room while the patient was being worked on. Serpico accompanied the prisoner to the surgical unit and observed the patient during anesthetization. Serpico was waiting for Mr. Ferraro in the recovery area and followed him to ICU. Serpico remained with Mr. Ferraro until I arrived in the ICU. I read Mr. Ferraro his rights as witnessed by Serpico and medical personnel. I am requesting permission to remand Paul Ferraro, aka Boston, to the custody of the FBI."

"Granted. Thank you for your assistance in this matter, Mr. Xavier." The director of the FBI turns her attention to the prisoner, "Mr. Ferraro, you have the right to remain silent…"

Manuel leaves the room, finds the nearest wall, slides the length of it and emotionally breaks.

Since arriving at the hospital, Granger Mitchell has been in a holding room with the body of a woman who he considered his daughter. He has been holding Stacy's hand every second that he has been with her. However, he doesn't hold his tears of loss and regret—couldn't if he tried.

When Fred comes to retrieve him, Granger places a lengthy kiss on Stacy's hand. He would prefer leaving that kiss on her forehead, but her injuries were ……. The shattered man rights himself with a deep breath and stands tall, "I love you, and I will miss you every day. No one has made me prouder than you have. You found that space in my heart that I had saved for you, only you, Stacy."

Attorney Granger Mitchell reaches into his pocket, removes one of his business cards and tucks it into Stacy's hand. "I gave you one of these on the day we met. I told you if you wrote to me I'd write back. There have been few things in this life of which I had been certain. Your writing to me was one of those things. You found my heart that day, Stacy. Seeing you here, like this, is breaking it."

Granger Mitchell gives one final kiss upon each of her fingers, folds them over his card, then walks away from the little girl from Harlem who grew up to become an incredible woman, one who made him a better man.

275

The RFI team enters the building through the back entrance a little after 8 AM. Mike demands that they assemble for a deconstruction of events. "I was watching inside the kitchen. Steve was watching the shooter. This is what I think went wrong."

A moan pushes from Steve, "Is this fucking necessary?"

"Necessary and protocol," Fred answers.

Mike continues. "Like the rest of us, Stacy could hear everything that Steve was saying. My best guess is that after she heard Steve say the shooter was ready for the shot, she overplayed the moment, or had second thoughts about Granger being there, or something hit in Stacy's mind that made her move to protect him— she stepped toward Granger just as the shot was made."

Steve gets up, addresses Fred, "I'm outta here. You gonna stop me?"

"Nope. Mike, continue."

"The height difference between Granger and Stacy turned a chest shot to Granger into a head shot to Stacy."

Steve hears those words before he makes it out of 275.

When the team disperses from the meeting, Manuel and Leavy head to Randy's empty apartment. She sits crossed legged on the bed; he sits on the floor, his back pressed into a corner. Silence hangs heavily until the ring of Manuel's cell phone disrupts it. The heartbroken man answers with one word, "Papa."

Rocco endures his son's pain for a moment, then tries to pull him back. "Manuel, your plan was solid and well-thought. I talked to Mike and heard his assessment; you should try to hear his words from the place outside your grieving heart. Manuel, what happened to Stacy is not your fault."

"I was in charge of the operation. It is my fault."

Rocco intentionally pushes his son. "Perhaps it's Steve's fault. Instead of telling everyone the shooter was taking the shot, Steve could have taken his own."

Manuel raises his voice to his father, "Steve did **nothing** wrong. He was keeping us in the moment by informing us of the events on the ground!"

"Ah, you are willing to defend Steve's actions and take responsibility for his judgments, but you are not willing to defend yourself. For now, you can take solace that your team members are doing that for you. Manuel, you are my son, and I know you will get to the truth of last night's events. I also know the path you choose to get to the truth is yours to find."

"But it's Stacy," Manuel breaks.

"Si, that is the real issue for you. She was your mentor, and she held an esteemed place in your life, rightfully so. That is a void that will stay with you. There is no point in trying to put your grief into a place where it makes sense—there is no such place, and no point in trying to hurry it along—it lives within its own measure of time. You know I speak from experience. Son, I am standing today because I learned that working through grief is the only option. Come home, Manuel. Learn that for yourself."

Fractured team.

Fred drives away from 275. When he arrives at the modified log cabin in Drexel Hill, he hasn't a single memory of making the trip. He sits a bit in the Jeep that belongs at this home, wondering where the hell he belongs at that very moment. He is pulled from his thoughts by Ted, who pushes into the passenger seat.

"You coming inside?"

"Not sure."

"Do you have something to say?"

"Not sure."

"I don't sit in Janelle's Jeep. Do you mind if we do whatever the fuck this is outside?"

The men step out. Ted leans back against the warm vehicle, "Fucking shit show last night," he snaps.

Fred nods, then kicks a rock on the front lawn that has captured his attention. He walks in its direction and kicks it again.

"What's happening at 275?"

Fred scoffs, and kicks. "Granger and Faye left not long after we returned from the hospital. They went out through the back alley. I think Granger spoke with Malcolm, but I don't really know for sure." Fred kicks the rock a few more times before continuing. "I have no idea how Granger is going to handle this. I'd share the story of how he and Stacy met, and what they've come to mean to one another, but it would crush the fuck out of you, so I'll save it for another time."

Ted nods, "I'd appreciate that. And Manuel, what's his status?"

"Fucked up. He's taking full responsibility, even though Mike did a deconstruction of events. He says he thinks when Stacy heard Steve's confirmation that the shooter was going to take the shot, she made a move to protect Granger. He says if Granger had been hit, it would have hit his Kevlar, but because of the height difference between the two, the chest hit for Granger became a fatal head shot for Stacy. Right now, Manuel isn't hearing any truth or logic."

"And Steve?"

"It'll be bad for him. He's got Stacy's blood on his hands, at least that's the way he's gonna process this."

"And you, Fred, how are you gonna process this?"

"Fuck if I know. I'm not even gonna pretend that I'm seeing anything clearly right now. Stacy Remington is a personal and professional loss that I'm gonna carry to my fucking grave, and it would have been that way even if I weren't part of the fuck up that got her killed."

Ted waits a moment while Fred chokes and pushes his pain down, then he walks halfway across his front lawn and grabs him tight.

Fred accepts the gesture, offers a thanks, and gets into the Jeep. He drives away without another word.

Ted enters his home to find Penny gone from the recliner. He finds her in his home office, "Hey, Lucky."

She turns and smiles, "Is that my new name?"

"Well, you did survive an assassination attempt."

She smiles wide. "I like it."

"Good. So, what are you doing up?"

"I could see you two through the window, and I just couldn't take it," she says through springing tears.

He opens his arms and let's his Lucky Penny step into them. Then he joins her in a tearful moment of his own.

275

Steve is gone from 275 when Fred returns. Mike hands him a note from their friend.

Rifles and ammunition are packed for the trip back to RFI.

Need time. See you on the flip side.

"You gonna give him time, or are you going after him?"

"Both. I know where he's going. I'll head in that direction, give some time, then get up in his shit." Fred packs his gear, "I'll be gone for a few days."

"What about Kitt? She's gonna need you to go back. And Maura, she just had the twins, she needs Steve," Mike states a whole bunch of obvious.

Fred shakes his head, "Our women aren't gonna be right until we get ourselves right. It sucks, but it's where we are right now. I hate to ask you to step up for us, Mike, but you're the only one who has a handle on this shit show. My advice to you is to lean on Annie for your emotional needs, and talk to Rocco, Joy, and John, about the professional end. They have years of experience handling this kind of shit. Don't forget they've all worked with and for Stacy, so you guys can be a help to one another. It's a fucking mess, Mike, but it is what it is."

The two men get the RFI gear into Malcolm's Land Rover for the trip to the airport. The jet is on standby for three passengers: Mike, Manuel and Leavy, and for two sniper rifles.

Fred gives Ted a call, "Steve is MIA. I think I know where he's heading."

"You've got the Jeep. Go find your partner."

"Appreciate it, Ted."

"Keep in touch. And Fred, while you're looking for Steve, take care of yourself."

Gretchen enters the great room just as the privacy elevator door is closing with Malcolm and part of the RFI team inside. Her husband bangs the door open button, "You need anything Woman?"

"Just wanted to say goodbye and to wish everyone a happy holiday."

Four sets of eyes share a look of confusion.

"Thanksgiving. It's tomorrow. I'm sure each of us has something to be thankful for." Gretchen stares blankly, then turns away, "Have a safe trip."

Broken marriage.

Malcolm returns to 275—alone. One step from the elevator and he knows he'll be staying that way. "Gretchen." He goes looking for his wife. He finds a note on her bedroom pillow.

Malcolm, I need some time.
I've moved into the guest suite.
I hope you will respect my choice. Gretchen

The End

More to come …

Please enjoy the teaser for my next book in the series, *Tests…*

TESTS

THE MEDIC

--- PULLING THREADS ---

Book Twelve

SHERYLL O'BRIEN

Malcolm

He stormed from their bedroom, down a hallway and through the adjoining space, dodging toolboxes, sawhorses, and construction debris left by a renovation crew. Walled off areas were starting to take shape — a nursery and playroom for his soon-to-be daughter — but nothing else in his life had shape anymore. **"Gretchen!"** the word echoed as he moved to the place where his wife had taken refuge. He balled the note she'd left and threw it from his hand.

The angry, advancing man stopped inches from the guest suite. He raised his fist to do some serious damage to the door — but lowered it when he realized that wasn't the barrier between them. Malcom unclenched his fist and placed his palm against the woodgrain. He lowered his head, his voice, "You need to set yourself right about me, Gretchen."

He turned and walked away.

Gretchen

She heard the tiny ping of the elevator seconds before she heard Malcolm call her name. When she didn't answer his call, she knew he'd check the bedroom and find the note she'd left on her pillow.

Malcolm, I need some time.
I've moved into the guest suite.
I hope you will respect my choice. Gretchen

The pregnant woman behind the closed door was staggered by her husband's building rage as he stormed through the penthouse – stunned by the heated emotion that owned the call of her name, **"Gretchen!"** It was all so unfamiliar. When she left the home they shared, she hoped her husband would give her the space she needed. She expected he would make his displeasure known – perhaps even demand she talk to him – listen to him.

She never thought he'd walk away.

ABOUT THE AUTHOR

She is not dead.

Sheryll O'Brien crafts characters without constraints. She tells them who they are, then let's them show her better versions of themselves. She gives them life and they live it beyond her wildest dreams.

Sheryll is a lifelong resident of Worcester, Massachusetts, where she is wife to the most supportive husband ever, and mother of two adult daughters, one who refuses to leave her home and the other who refuses to tell her where she lives. Of most significance, she is MammyGrams to the sweetest six-year-old, Hadley.

Sheryll worked several years in the fundraising community of Worcester County, writing grants for non-profit organizations. She began writing for her own pleasure after surviving brain surgery and breast cancer. Happily, for her fanbase of family and friends-—she is not dead.

If you have enjoyed reading my book, I would very much appreciate you taking a few minutes to write a review and post that review on amazon.com and goodreads.com.

The opinion of readers can help prospective readers make a purchasing decision.

To learn more, please visit my website, www.pullingthreadsnovella.com subscribe to my blog for updates on future projects.

I would absolutely love to hear from my readers, you can email me at,

pullingthreadsnovella@gmail.com

www.ingramcontent.com/pod-product-compliance
Lightning Source LLC
LaVergne TN
LVHW010057110826
845155LV00028B/373

* 9 7 8 1 9 3 9 3 5 1 3 0 2 *